BEYOND THE BRACKETS

A COLLECTION OF WORKS

BY

THE NOM DE PLUMES OF CHESHIRE

DEDICATION

ALEX WATSON

This Anthology is dedicated to our recently deceased friend, Alex, who was a member of our Writing Group. He was a real gentleman who, along with his warm personality, possessed a delightfully dry sense of humour.

This book contains a small selection of his creative work.

CONTENTS

NIGHTS IN WHITE SATIN

ALEX WATSON

It's an education in life, this job of mine. Not only do I see parts of the country most of my Cheshire neighbours shun, but I meet the sort of people they avoid with a shudder. Last week's care quality inspection was at Sunshine House in a Newcastle suburb. Between you and me, it wasn't my first choice of assignment. I am a bit uncomfortable around the elderly as they remind me of the ageing process. I like to think I am particularly vigilant in care homes as I see myself as a future resident.

I knew that Sunshine House was in the same complex as Benton Community Hospital. I couldn't find the home. I asked the community hospital receptionist for directions.

Folding her arms across her chest, she informed me, 'It's not a good time gannin' there. They're havin' their dinna.'

Lunchtime was perfect for me. The staff would be fully stretched. Although forewarned of my arrival, they would now be expecting me after lunch.

When I found the care home, I could see why it was hidden from plain sight. It might well have won awards for brutalism. There was no welcome sign. I rang the bell and a young, spotty faced man answered my summons.

'Hello, miss,' he said.

'Hello. I'm Rachael Petrie from the Care Quality Commission.' He nodded, but did not give me his name.

'Anyway, I assume you are expecting me?' He nodded again. 'Well, if you could take me your manager.'

He turned and started walking down a corridor and made no attempt at small talk. I had to hurry to keep pace with him. I made a mental note to ask what inter-personal relationship training the staff received. My first impressions of the décor were favourable, but at that speed I could not be certain.

I was pondering whether an abstract painting was hung the right way up, when my guide abruptly stopped. Without knocking, he pushed open a door to a bedroom. Swallowing my irritation, I merely repeated my request to see the manager. Saying nothing, he bent over and took off his shoes and then gestured I do the same. I had never been asked to do this before. Was this care home policy, or the wish of the (surely female) occupant?

I was curious to see what lay within this house-proud lady's room. I took off my shoes and went inside. The young man followed and closed the door. He then took a jay cloth from his pocket and started cleaning the doorknob. The door closing and knob cleaning made me a little uneasy.

He opened all the drawers in the room. I hadn't planned to invade the resident's privacy in this way and made another mental note. He then opened the wardrobe. I was greeted with the sight of seven corsets arranged in rainbow order, from flaming red to voluptuous violet. Also on the rack were three brilliant white corsets. What sort of woman lived here? I then noticed there was not one dress, one blouse or one skirt. The wardrobe only contained corsets. Something was not right, not right at all.

His next action heightened my unease. He lay down on the bed and beckoned to me to do likewise. I shook my head vigorously. Clearly disappointed, he spoke for the first time since the entrance. 'Soft,' he said, 'lovely and soft.' He patted the bed.

I moved over to the safety of the wardrobe and pointed at the lemon corset. 'I don't wear corsets, but I love this colour.'

His countenance changed instantly. He snarled 'Stoopid. Stoopid. It's a satin basque from Agent Provocateur. A basque, stoopid!'

How did he know that? How did he know the make? His eyes locked into mine. He rose from the bed and crossed to the wardrobe. I feared the worst but he ignored me. He picked the basque from the rail and caressed the garment as if it had been violated. All at once it came to me. This was his basque. These were his loved possessions. This was his room.

He started to talk to the lingerie as a young girl might talk to her stuffed animals. I sighed from relief. He was harmless. I was still puzzled about his presence in a care home for the elderly.

I had to find the manager now. I made for the door, but it wouldn't open. The young man hadn't locked it - had he? I spotted an orange cord and tugged the bell for assistance. I tried the door once more. He started to cry, loud heart-wrenching sobs. I confess that I didn't wait to comfort him. I gave the door an almighty shove and I left. I ran straight into an angry woman in a business suit.

'What are you doing in Moonshine House?' She glared. Loud wails came from the young man's room. 'You've upset, Robbie.' She shouted at a colleague, 'Don't let that one leave,' she commanded, pointing at me. She hurried into Robbie's room.

This colleague looked like a professional wrestler or a prison warder. I stood in front of her in an unaggressive manner. Inside I was seething for I knew I was innocent.

After five minutes, the manager returned. She was still incandescent but I remained calm. Through her words of vitriol, I gradually assembled a clearer picture. Firstly, I was not in Sunshine House, but in Moonshine House which took care of young adults with various mental disorders. Both facilities shared a common entrance hall. The manager conceded that the signage was inadequate.

Robbie had multiple disorders. He was obsessively tidy, hence the need for us to remove our shoes, and he was passionate to excess about his lingerie collection. Each night, bar Sundays, he wore a white satin corset. On the Sabbath, he selected one of the rainbow basques. Robbie was so self-centered he thought that my inspection was solely to praise his undies. My words and actions were an attack on his world.

I have been assured that Robbie has fully recovered from our encounter. How I wish I had heeded the receptionist's advice: 'It's not a good time gannin' there.'

The End

THE CONTROLLING SUN

ROBYN CAIN

The controlling sun enticed Nick outside. Grinning evilly, it soon drove him to shelter under the spread arms of the resplendent apple tree.

Sighing satisfactorily at the lush and heavy, sweet smelling perfection around him, Nick opened his heavy tome and began to read.

Several hours in, he summoned his wife. She served him crisps, individually wrapped cake bars and cheese strings, which he munched with sips of cool drinks from cardboard cartons lined with non-recyclable plastic. The book was boring and soon had him yawning, then napping.

*

A rustling, a fluttering, a thump on his head from a falling apple, and Nick is awake. Making a fist he kicks the unmovable base. Further dissatisfied, he yells and gives the tree a shake, but it retaliates by cascading more fruit his way. Now he has a head that aches.

Sun howls with laughter at Nick's enraged yowls.

Nick shouts to his wife for an axe. She replies, 'Don't do that, dear. Mind your stress levels. Remember what the doctor said.' Nevertheless, she goes off to do as told because he's gone red.

Mutinously, he hurls the beautiful, round, tangy fruit out of sight when the sharp, glistening tool arrives.

'Come and watch,' Sun calls to his friends.

As breeze-blown clouds skip along and delight tautly strung kites, the heavens watch Nick chop, and grin at the blisters on his soft hands rising to be popped. Whacking, smashing, cracking, the dying tree's branches stir and unsettle nesting birds, while all around those who can look, do, and sigh, 'What a tosser!'

Fiery-faced Sun challenges Wind to churn up a storm, uproot the foliage and tear at the lawn, raising the book which flicks and trips up the man. Sight and judgment impaired, the perfectly poised, glinting axe cuts into Nick – and he is split from skull to chin.

The End

RED SKY

ROSALIE ROSS

The year is 1970. The setting is a crowded hotel dining room somewhere in the Scottish Highlands. The atmosphere is convivial and relaxed - apart from the vicinity around a centre table where three people sit waiting for the fourth member of their party.

Twenty minutes had passed and still there was no sign of Sky McLoud, the lead vocalist of the popular Starold Star Ceilidh Band who were staying overnight in the hotel.

Georgina MacMan, one of the hotel's owners, had waited long enough. She had taken her time with the fruit juice and felt herself being sorely tempted by the sight and smells of the main courses being delivered to the tables nearby. She watched how one man eagerly tucked into a steaming plate of bashed neeps and haggis, and it was all she could do not to announce that she, for one, intended to 'place her order within the next two minutes, come what may.' Turning to the youthful looking percussionist to her right, she exclaimed, 'Why don't you run along and see what the delay is? Do tell her that we're extremely busy tonight.'

The man calmly stared back at the imperious figure, but remained seated. He was well used to his colleague's tardiness and had learned to make full use of his naturally patient disposition. Placing both hands on the table in front of him, he began to tap out a quick rhythm as he replied, 'No need. She'll be along right enough; that one's all for making a grand entrance.'

'Aye,' added the equally becalmed and pragmatic piper sitting beside him, ponderously stroking his long grey beard. 'That one'll be here, but only when she's good and ready.'

Georgina took the final, orangey sip and sighed heavily. 'Well, okay. But it really is *too* bad of her. And I'll need to be finished in here...' However, she was prevented from listing all the things she needed to get done before being able to escape up to the flat, when a piercing shriek emanated from somewhere behind her, causing her to almost drop her glass. Spinning around, she was just in time to see the kitchen swing doors fly open to reveal a truly alarming sight. For there, with Frazier the chef following hot on its heels, appeared such a shocking apparition that she had to force herself to believe what she was seeing, as the unearthly, banshee-type spectacle flew past her.

A woman, dressed in a long, flowing, elaborately decorated black and red silk kimono - under which flashes of a neon-pink, ultra-short petticoat could be glimpsed - began making her noisy and blundering way through the tables. Enormous sponge pink rollers covered her head, and a badly cracked white face pack masked her horrified and terrified countenance. But it was what was attached to one of her flailing arms that eventually fixed everyone's eye. For there, clamped vice like, was a very menacing looking black shiny object.

The screeching and screaming - Georgina couldn't quite distinguish the difference, even though she could detect two distinct tones - continued as the spectre made its noisy progress through the dumbstruck diners.

Standing by the bar, Donald managed at last to control his shock and decided that something needed to be done pretty smartly to stop the rumpus. Carefully laying down his full tray, he saw his chance when the awful thing stormed past him. Reaching out, he grabbed the crustacean-free arm and stood his ground, bringing it unceremoniously to an abrupt and clumsy halt. Immediately behind, Frazier succeeded in grabbing the figure under the other arm and attempted, but failed, to free the evening's specialty from its clinging situation with his other. At last, on the third courageous attempt, and despite all the continuous violent shaking, the pair managed to eject the still noisy phenomenon from the public arena and back into the more private confines of the kitchen. Discreet, small bursts of relieved laughter began to ripple around the dining room as a succession of whimpers and loud sobs began to sound from behind the swing doors.

The percussionist and piper stared hard at each other. They were used to the antics of their flamboyant band member, but this latest debacle was off even her dramatic scale. What could one say after witnessing such an event? What excuse could they offer now?

'Looks like lobster's off the menu then,' commented the latter, beginning to softly whistle the melodic strains of *The Sky Boat Song* between his clenched teeth.

*

Yvonne had been descending the staff stairs when she heard the commotion coming from below. Rushing through the kitchen and into the dining room, she was amazed to behold the incongruous sight of Donald and Frazier struggling with an hysterical figure who seemed to be attempting to throw some long black object around. She stood, frozen to the spot, staring hard, as the men finally managed to free the thing from its ghastly human host.

Donald's forehead was covered with beads of sweat as, breathing heavily, he turned to her and beseeched her to escort the mortified, supremely embarrassed, and now furious woman, back to her room and do what she could to restore peace and order to their shattered lives.

*

Needless to say, and much to everyone's relief, Sky McLoud did not make any more appearances that night, spectacular or otherwise.

Frazier told them later that she had walked around the back of the Inn and popped her head through the kitchen door, and asked him, 'To take a wee look to see if that nice Alexander Grant has arrived.' Whereupon, he replied that 'He was far too busy to be doing any such thing!'

Not used to such treatment, she flounced impatiently past him, causing one of her gown's voluminous sleeves to fly much too close to the large pan on the hob. She had then flown into a wild panic when she felt, and saw, what had managed to attach itself onto her person, and dashing past him, crashed through the swing doors and into the dining room.

*

The trio left very early the next morning. They had not breakfasted, but had instead requested extra Rich Tea biscuits with their early morning drinks. Yvonne couldn't help noticing how very red Sky's face looked when she took her tray in, even in the room's semi-gloom.

Later that day, pen in hand, Georgina paused over her *Little Black Book.* She was having second thoughts about adding the band's name to *The Black List*, after all, they were well thought of in these parts. But, then again, some of their material was a touch too coarse for her taste. And didn't she overhear someone remark that they were a little pricey?

Her decision made, she began to write in her precise, neat hand:-

The Starold Star Ceilidh Band. Extreme caution.
Miss Sky prone to highly embarrassing
public displays of exhibitionism.

The End

I'm Carrying a Tumour

Alex Watson

I'm carrying a tumour, I'm praying it's not quins.
Just one's a blasted nuisance, I'm dreading even twins.
We're discussing every option, but really there is one.
Au naturel's unheard of, and all the baths have gone
Private.

They're doing a Caesarean, more Brutal than it sounds.
Procedure's antiquarian, throwing offal on the ground.
But with a Good Samaritan to put me off to sleep
For an operation marathon.
Then he'll haul me up from deep
Intoxication.

I'm carrying a tumour but when delivery's o'er
I'll wake up in a sunlit ward and ask the doc the score
At St James's Park

*

MOUSTACHE

RUBY WELLINGTON

I didn't notice the onset of the moustache until it had fully arrived. However, it must have always been there, although in a softer, subtler form.

I looked at the upper lip of my co-workers, paying particular attention to those on the advent of, or who were post-menopause, to see if they too had any signs, but could detect none; which could only mean that they must have found a way of dealing with them.

My colleague, Janet, of course, goes regularly to a salon where she has a *boy* who plucks, tweaks and dyes various parts of her body. I'm sure the same *boy* prepares the transvestites for the local cabaret.

I scurry off to the shops and discover a choice of three methods of removal: shaving, waxing or creaming. Even though there is the advert for the first choice, I refuse to shave my face. Oh, they don't call the gadget a *shaver,* but that's what it actually is. It conjures up all sorts of childhood images of my father shaving in the living room – that familiar buzzing sound and all those facial contortions – and *then* emptying the contents onto the carpet.

As I hand over my merchandise, the young cashier asks me if I have a *loyalty* card, to which I reply with my standard comment, 'No, I don't believe that the word *loyalty* and shopping should be in the same sentence.'

She looks at me as if I am weird, and replies, 'Well, you don't only have to shop with us, you know!'

I bag my wax buys and feel as if I have become part of an undercover world that unites women. Then I wonder what is the purpose of the moustache? It must have one because everything does. Perhaps its job is to collect germ particles and prevent them from being breathed in? Nature has fantastic balance. In which case, I should leave it alone to do its job.

There is so much expected of us women; it appears that the majority use dyes to avoid grey or dull coloured hair. In addition to what I have already mentioned, there is the plucking, teeth whitening, the scary nail craze, and the regular trips to the underwear department for bra fittings. Age has not only changed my body without warning, but also my breasts. Now my bra has to act like a hoist as well as offering support. Soft, feminine lacy bras are replaced with unforgiving, firm, scaffolding structures. And I haven't even ventured into the world of support underwear.

What happened to the ideals of feminism? Perhaps it's time to re-launch the burn your bra and go native campaign?

As I cross the car park, I notice an old neighbour who recently moved into sheltered accommodation. We stop to face each other under the unforgiving glare of a street light, and I see that the woman has a beard. Good for her, I think, quietly congratulating her courage – and knowing that I'll be waxing my face later that evening.

The End

'WILL YOU TAKE THIS MAN?'

HEBE GREEN

Janie breathed in as she examined herself in the full-length mirror and decided that she didn't look too bad at all. She turned and glanced at the blue sky outside; a perfect day for a wedding. She felt the anticipation of seeing Beatrice, Rosie, and Sally again, the three good friends she hadn't seen for a while; everyone was always so busy or on holiday. Beatrice's daughter was getting married; the couple had lived together for two years and were now making a firm commitment.

Everything's strange these days, she thought, adjusting her shoes and beginning to apply her make-up; things were all back to front. Still, I suppose it gives them time to change their minds, better than having a divorce, which was something she knew all about and wouldn't recommend to anybody.

After thirty years of marriage and two children, Steve had run off with his young secretary. Old story, very corny. She had gone down four dress sizes and had become almost anorexic, which was slightly ironic, as for most of her life she had been on one diet or another. She had hated him so much it hurt. How she had cursed him for destroying the family, and then blamed herself for not being how he wanted her, although that didn't last for long as everyone soon started to blame him. She forbade the children to talk about him and wouldn't listen to anything they had to say when they returned after visiting him down south.

In time, she had picked herself up, dusted herself down, and started all over again – as the old song put it. She had returned to college and trained as a nurse, eventually becoming a ward sister. These days she went to the gym twice a week and was now a neat size twelve. She may be in her fifties, but she certainly didn't look it. She had *made it,* and all by herself, and she was proud of the fact. She was still alone by choice; no man would ever get near enough to hurt her again. If she was honest, she still loved Steve, although she would never admit it to anybody. And she was glad that he wasn't around to hurt her anymore.

*

The church was crowded. After the initial hugs and greetings, she went to join Rosie and Sally and their husbands near the back to survey the colourful variety of hats and other finery. The moment arrived for the vows. Janie strained to see if Beatrice was shedding a tear – and that was when she saw him, sitting several rows in front. Steve! Her stomach lurched and she could feel her heart beating faster. How on earth had she missed seeing him? She was shocked at her feelings – and after all this time, after the way she had built her emotional wall so carefully, brick by brick. From what she could see of him, back here, he looked as though he hadn't changed much, maybe a little greyer. Then she remembered that he'd been Beatrice's husband's best friend back in the old days. But why hadn't Beatrice told her and given her time to prepare herself?

Totally shaken, she was trembling, and feeling insecure again. Somehow, she *must* pull herself together. She found herself hiding behind the big hats and chattering to people when the smiling, kissing couple made their slow way down the aisle. She didn't want to see him with *that* woman - holding hands and happy, maybe even still in love. She didn't want him to feel sorry for her. 'Anyway, I don't care!' she muttered, then realised she was talking aloud.

'What was that, did you say something?' asked Sally, turning to face her. 'Are you alright? You look a little pale.'

'I'm fine, Sal, thanks. Just had a blast from the past, that's all.' She managed to grin as she nodded over to Steve's direction.

'Oh my goodness!' gasped Sally. 'We never thought he'd turn up. Not in a million years!'

'What?' asked Janie. 'You knew he'd be here? And you never told me?'

Sally looked a little shamefaced. 'We didn't think he'd come. He didn't answer the invitation...so we thought...but Dave insisted on inviting him. Remember, he was his best mate before all...' She trailed off, not knowing what else to say and feeling sad for Janie. 'And Dave said it happened so long ago...you wouldn't mind. Beatrice couldn't talk him out of it, so we were just relieved when he didn't reply.'

Sally's expression made Janie feel sorry for her. She gave her a quick hug. After all, it wasn't her fault, and it was no reason for the whole day to be ruined.

They all went out into the brilliant sunshine. Janie went to hide until all the photographs were over, she needed to ground herself and get back to feeling strong again. However, the others soon found her and wouldn't hear of her excuses when she tried to get out of going on to the hotel where the reception was being held.

*

The friends had all booked for an overnight stay so they could chill out and drink without worrying about driving home. They were in Rosie's room. 'Come on, let's put them on the bill,' laughed Rosie, draining her glass. 'It's great ringing for room service, isn't it?' It was like any other time when they got together. They had supported and cried with each other, like the time Rosie had breast cancer, celebrating when she had the all-clear and her hair had grown back again. They'd had a weekend away just for the hell of it.

They adjourned to the reception sometime later, all slightly tipsy. Beatrice wanted to apologise to Janie and managed to have a quiet word with her. 'I just couldn't make Dave see that you'd still be upset.'

'Well, he is a man,' shrugged Janie, 'So I suppose you can't blame him.'

Soon, the speeches were in full flow, but Janie wasn't listening, she was trying to steal a look at the woman beside Steve. She couldn't quite make out who she was. The last time she had seen them together was when they left in the car. What a moment that had been. She and Steve had been a couple since they were eighteen, how on earth could that woman come and spoil all that? She never thought it possible to hate somebody so much.

At last, the speeches were over. She went to change into the little black dress that always made her feel good. She stared in the full-length mirror and knew she looked great. Now she was glad that she hadn't let herself go. And Steve would see that she still cared about herself – if he didn't. She felt ready to go down and face her fears, to face him and that woman with him - and get rid of his ghost forever.

There was a knock at the door. Steve stood there, smiling. Shocked, she stared at him.

'Hello Janie. They…er, told me where you were.
I wanted to talk to you alone. Can I come in?'

Seconds passed and all her resolve faded as feelings came rushing at her.

He shut the door behind him. 'I'm sorry Janie, more than I can ever say. I never wanted to hurt you. I never wanted to hurt anyone. I'm so sorry.'

She wanted him to go, but still couldn't speak as he held her hand and told her that he'd been a total fool, that his girlfriend had moved out years ago and that he hadn't had anyone since. Only now did he have the courage to tell her. He continued pouring his heart out and sounded so sincere that she began to believe him. The old trust started to come back and she was even prepared to think about giving him a second chance.

*

The others were amazed and pleased when they eventually joined them. Whatever Janie decided was good enough for them, and they had hated her being alone all these years.

Steve stayed the night. It was as if they had never been apart as she lay in his arms and realised that the forgiving wasn't going to be that hard. She wondered if she should have played a little harder to get, but she was happy to be part of a couple again. And she had to admit that she did still love him.

Steve was pleased with himself and very, very relieved that he wouldn't have to go through the ordeal alone now.

He would have to choose his time carefully about when to tell her about the cancer.

Definitely not now, not yet. Tomorrow maybe? Or the day after…

The End

LOCKED EXPOSURE

ROBYN CAIN

She was a conversation piece. At work, down her street and even family gatherings – she was the topical topic. When she reached that certain age when life began again, it was decided she had to be helped. She had to be saved from cruel conversations with Machiavellian Time, who once, in the past, had given her a little taste of love and then taken it away.

It took a lot of persuading, but finally she saw she was lonely. When she met the man they exchanged one kiss that lit the fuse and chemistry began to do its work. But when he took her hand she pulled back and hid behind her old ways.

The man thought up a plan. He went to the shop where they sold clever lenses and said to the owner, 'The camera's eye has to be detailed. The battle is imminent. I have to save her.'

'Then this is the camera you need,' the shop owner told the man. 'It has a cruel eye. Like a weapon, it will touch everything, and pass over nothing. It will prettify and Photoshop nothing. It ignores not one iota of minutia. It will be relentless as it consumes in order to regurgitate and fight for your corner.'

'That's the camera I must have,' the man said. 'It has to be relentless. Unrecoverable years have already passed by for her.'

Considering her worth saving, the man inveigled the camera into the unwary woman's life.

Machiavellian Time liked to hold onto stale breath. Like trapped wind, Time sourced its power from emotions. It especially liked mocking humans with their ever-changing, foundation-less plans and never-to-be-reached deadlines. Time's outright laughter affected the air and disturbed psyches. When it hovered around them, making them wince, it also brought to the fore a certain dogged determinism to stay and fight; a brave facade helped when evacuation wasn't an option. Time liked the taste of aphrodisiacal power over the woman. It had become his daily fix, and he reveled in the mockery and pity afforded from those with knowledge of her life, especially the reducing effect it had upon her.

Time had met the camera before.

When it was done, the camera gave the thumbs up to indicate it had consumed all it needed.

The woman was a little afraid of the forthcoming battle for change, but the man reassured her, 'It never lies. And the truth, although painful, will make everything good.'

On the big day the woman opened the front door and let both Time and the man in.

Time spoke, 'You haven't changed. You've done nothing to change. Ergo, you won't change.'

The astute man quickly replied, 'Determinism. She's no longer alone. Two are stronger.'

'Isms! Mathematics! Really?' exclaimed Time. 'Opportunities have come and she's let them go.' Glaring at the woman, he instructed, 'Look into the camera's exposure.'

The woman answered, 'We have before. We're a unit. He's made a commitment. He's made a change.'

'All evidence to the contrary. Delusional female. There's no change,' said Time.

'There is. *Me.* And I'm opening the curtains. Letting in the light,' the man replied. 'And I've got her back. And she's mine.'

'Not from where I'm standing. And unlike you, I've known her since her first wail.' Looking down at the seated woman, Time laughed because she was absorbed, staring at the computer screen and totally immobile. *'You can lead a horse to water...* and all that, but can you make it drink?'

'At least I'll have tried,' the man said bravely although inside he felt worried.

'Tick tock,' said Time, knowing that he had conquered yet again. He winked at the man before sliding out of the house through the gap under the door.

The End

DELL-ILAH'S DILEMMA

ROSALIE ROSS

Dell-ilah paused to look out of the window. A large cloud obscured her view. She quickly launched herself into her landscape and began compressing the rubbish in her recycle bin, making room for all those nasty little biting bits she knew would come cascading down at any microsecond. Returning, she sighed and thought what an awful month it had been. Ever since installing that last set of updates she had been feeling more sluggish than ever. All she had wanted to do was refresh her wardrobe and try out a few of those new and attractive accessories. How she would love to customise and realign her self-image and keep up with those smart Hewlett Packard's and IBM's! They were so trim and toned and always excelled in displaying their fine qualities. And now those new fancy Surface Pros were on the scene, what chance did an old piece of hardware like her have?

She modified her position, causing a memory to flip onto her consciousness. It was of that miserable night she had attended the Style Guide Function. How she managed to navigate her way to the Fizzy Font Bar after that embarrassing episode with Andy Acer and Tommy Toshiba's hotkeys, she never knew. And it didn't help when that bitchy Alison Apple had got on her pip by boasting about her fancy new dual-core processor.

No wonder she had choked over the jam and spam sandwiches. At least Sammy Sony had cheered them all up by announcing that he had decided to stop being so remote and link up with Mandy Microsoft, although how he would cope with such a digitally dizzy hyper piece who did nothing but zip around the place, she had no idea! Apparently, they had been emailing each other for a while and were expecting to merge any time now.

'Hi there, Dell. My word, WhatsApp?' boomed a loud voice from somewhere nearby. 'You're looking a bit low. Been doing too much tweeting and twittering again, have you?'

Oh no! The Operator had put that awful Deeper Blue next to her. That's all she needed, this smug, big-headed supercomputer, trying to connect with her at a time like this. It was okay for him with all his fancy petabyte bits. But she liked to take things a bit slower. Well, she had no choice, did she, being stuck with just one measly terabyte. Deeper was such a fast piece, so shifty, always spying around and behaving as though he was the mainframe leader of the pack. Who had given him the authority to challenge the Operator anyway? Trying to divert things a bit, she right clicked and put a call out for BusB, her pet mousepad, and asked if he fancied going for a stroll. Too late, she remembered he was hibernating; now she would have to put up with this mega pain.

'Well, if you must know, I think I've picked up some sort of virus,' she replied, indignantly.

'What a drag!' he sneered, beginning to inch away, although he wasn't too concerned; he was far too superior to cache any common virus. 'Dropped you in it, has he?' he asked, referring sarcastically to the Operator, which he always did whenever any of them had a problem. 'You really should listen to my advice and let me lighten your load. Let me relieve you of those nasty old memories. We don't need *his* help; I can do it in a flash, and you won't even feel a thing.'

Grrr! Why didn't he change his tune? He was always after her data, and even had the nerve recently to hint that he wouldn't mind connecting with her hyperlinks! But he just wasn't her type, even though it was true that she had been quite font of him once. Shifting her view, she replied testily, 'No, clear off!' A sudden twinge in her back warned her that her old floppy disc problem was threatening again. 'I'm not in the mood for any of your antics.'

'Tut-tut! You really must learn to control your emoticons. You sound full of them. Oh well, much as I'd like to assist you and all that, I'll have to get going. My task manager's queuing up and wants me to spy out some new layouts for three new properties I've just registered for. Now, why don't you be a good little girl and hibernate for a while and preserve what little usefulness you've got left. Anyway, must rush. Bye for now.'

She watched his massive frame shrink as he made a quick exit. Well, despite that nasty twinge, there was work to do. She instructed Kody, her faithful old printer, to start spooling, but he began spouting some weird symbols. Totally fed-up now, she wondered if a spot of exercise might help, and decided to go for quick surf. However, she wasn't able to move fast enough and ended-up getting so cold that she froze solid. Desperation overwrote her, if only she could escape to some far away port. There were so many exotic sounding game and film sites out there that she hadn't visited yet. But she knew it was power-pointless; she had already spent hours fruitlessly skyping for a new lifecycle. And now she had even started to think the unthinkable - and switch her internet service provider! Seeking comfort, she dipped into her vast store of chips and cookies.

'Hello! Don't be alarmed,' came a cheerful voice from a work station somewhere nearby. 'I've been informed that you've been feeling a bit drained lately.'

Oh no! Not another one of those bossy boot antivirally thingies she was always trying to avoid. She couldn't stand it. Half closing her lid, she began to close down.

'It's okay. I'm only here to help you,' the voice said in a comforting mode.

Curious, she lifted her view and restarted. A dazzling, but somehow weird and wonderful aura seemed to be surrounding her. She blinked and googled at the stranger. What was he? He couldn't be...could he? He must be. How wonderful! 'Golly! Hello! Are you a wizard?' she asked, hopefully.

'No. I'm a doctor. I'm called Auxilium, and one of my functions is to do house-calls to help the sick.'

She did a double right click and flashed her rather depleted lashes at him. What a surprise! A doctor! Thinking about it, that's just what she needed. 'Oh good! Who sent you? Was it one of my friends? Was it Katy Kindle? That would be just like her; she's so thoughtful.'

'No, the Operator sent me. Now just lay back and let me see what's been going on. I wouldn't be surprised if you've had a visit from my arch enemy, Trojan. He's been causing chaos around here lately. A very nasty piece of work.'

'Actually, now you mention it, I do feel kind of defragmented. Do you think I've caught this Trojan thing then? And, if so, why's he picked on me? I've never done anyone any harm.'

'Well, you know, everyone's at risk,' Auxilium said, his light beginning to permeate through her spaces, giving her a cosy, warm feeling. 'And the only way to avoid catching infections like him is to be willing to accept my help - my protection.'

'Protection? Hm.' She wasn't so sure about that. Now he was starting to sound like one of those antivirally thingies after all. Disappointed, she said defensively, 'I've always used what my dear old motherboard had, and it was good enough for her.'

'But you're your own person and have to make your own choices. Your motherboard can't help you now. I'm afraid there's no shortcut you can take for this one. And, actually, I've been doing a quick scan on you as we've been dialoging, and it looks like your Firewall's been doused. No wonder you've been feeling out of sorts. I really do need to perform a deep scan on you. Do I have your permission?'

Still Dell-ilah wasn't convinced, even though there was something very appealing about this one. But a girl had to be sure. 'Er, well, I don't let just anyone mess around with my protocols, you know,' she replied, cautiously. 'And I'm pretty fussy about my temporary and sub-folders. And I'm not sure I like the idea of you delving into all my lovely old archived bits. How do I know that you won't go creating any new files without my permission, or even posting personal things about me on social media?'

'Rest assured. I won't do any of that,' he replied, glowing quietly away.

Dell-ilah thought hard as she chewed her recently varnished jpegs.

The visitor allowed her a full sixty seconds to ponder, then said, 'Please don't be alarmed, but I have to go along your roots and down into the core of your being. Nothing must stay hidden from me. It's only by being willing to open yourself up and let me in that you can be truly delivered from everything that's been ruining your life. Then your Operator can re-install all the corrupt parts and re-create you to be the lovely, healthy computer he designed you to be.'

Dell-ilah felt her up arrow key, which had been badly depressed lately, begin to quiver into life, and somehow she recognised that this strange new machine was telling her the truth. He had such a calm and reassuring mode about him. Maybe she would be foolish to refuse him access to her and customise her back into the speedy girl she had once been. Taking a deep breath, she capitulated.

'Well, I suppose I have been a bit off-colour lately and… if you really can help. Oh, go on then. Just give me a second.' It took her a while to remember how to do it, but at last she succeeded, and allowed the nice looking piece of hardware to control her remotely.

'Alright. Well done. Stand by!' Auxilium responded, immediately getting to work. Soon, he had efficiently navigated his way through her plethora of web pages, websites, applications, blurred windows and WinZip's; he whizzed effortlessly through her WordPad, Wordbook and crowded Word programme, until, at last, he arrived safely at the required destination.

Impatient as ever, Dell-ilah felt that the macro-minutes were passing by too slowly, and was tempted to press her start button to stop him. Then she remembered that a few of her tiles had some nasty chips in them. Maybe she should make good use of the time and do a spot of decorating? But Auxilium must have been keeping tabs on her, because when she tried to mix some paste, he popped up and asked her to cut it out. Knowing she was beaten, she began to doze…

*

'Dell-ilah, Dell-ilah! Wake up girl! Time to put those boots back on.'

Someone, far away, was calling her name. She blinked into life. She felt dazed and not quite herself.

'Greetings!' the stranger said, flashing some wonderful colours at her. 'Welcome back! Have you had a good sleep?'

She focused on him, and replied, groggily, 'I…I feel like I've been f-a-ar away for a l-o-ong time. Like I've been sort of…hibernating. What…what happened?'

Wiping a few drops of sweat from his handsome screen, Auxilium replied, 'You caught a nasty bug. Your core was so badly corrupted that I had to wipe away a lot of your history and reinstall your good memories.'

'Oh dear! Goodness me!' she whimpered, obviously overcome with the enormity of it all.

'But don't worry, you're still you. Only a much healthier version of yourself now that you've been fully restored. I found Trojan. That nasty devil! But I uprooted and sorted him out alright. He's in a good, strong quarantine cell and can't hurt you anymore.'

Reassured at last, she exclaimed, 'Oh thank you! Thank you. How can I ever repay you?'

'My pleasure, and my services are free. But it's the Operator you should really be thanking.'

'I will! Oh, I will!' she exclaimed, full of emoticons.

'Good. I'm pleased to hear it. You know, he's been trying to dialogue with you ever since you arrived, but you've been ignoring him.'

'Have I? How foolish of me. What could I have been thinking?'

'What indeed! Anyway, from now on you must make sure that he's the *only* one you allow to press your control key. And when he presses the arrow keys and tells you to go up, don't go down! Don't go to the left when he wants you to go to the right. Otherwise you'll end up falling back into your old ways. Co-operate with him when he wants to do some housework and routine maintenance on you. Keep on reminding yourself that your home's been cleansed with his forgiveness and that you're fully justified. Now you're free to function according to your original design. And another thing, always make sure you're protected when you go browsing and window shopping.'

'Didn't I used to?' she queried, somewhat surprised.

'No. I'm afraid you didn't.'

'Oh dear! I'm so sorry. How very foolish of me.'

'It's alright. I've…taken all the damage away from you and dealt with it. The Operator's forgiven you now. But always remember that all he wants to do is to help and support you, and that all his commands are for your good. I'd like to hear that you're building a brand new history for yourself. So take care when you associate with any machine that habitually overwrites their ideas on others.

Especially beware of the ones that worship false icons; I'm afraid there's a lot of them around. Anyway, you're all set-up and ready to go now.'

She felt so refreshed, and resolving to live this new, healthier life, took a deep breath, and pressed *<Enter>*. Immediately a surge of power went through her. Then some long forgotten sensations came flooding in: brilliant thoughts, exciting ideas, and wonderful programmes. All clean, all organised, and such *quality!* She beamed as a bold, new message appeared in glorious shades across her screen: SAVED.

Auxilium was satisfied. He had done his work well; the little one was safe now. All her colour had returned: vivid, clear, and beautiful. He began to collect his files together.

Curious, she put a call through to her dictionary and asked what the name Auxilium meant. The answer came back immediately: *Auxilium: Latin for The Helper.*

'Well, I'd better be going,' he said, closing, clicking and locking his briefcase before hurrying away to respond to yet another emergency, calling over his shoulder as he did so, 'Remember now, follow the Operator's plan for you, and you'll have a far happier and worthwhile lifespan!'

'I'll remember,' she called back, already logging onto her Century Gothic newsgroup, eager to read all the latest gossip, and feeling very safe as she did so. But, what was this? A large heading popped up, making her do a double left click.

'FAREWELL TO OUR LOCAL SUPERCOMPUTER'

Eager to discover what this was all about, she pressed some keys so fast that they became hot as, without a pause, she read on. Beeps sounded from her newly tuned speaker when she learned the terrible news that little Annie Amstrad had been seriously damaged after allowing some of her precious, historically unique files to be transferred over to the supercomputer. However, in the supercomputer's overconfident haste, he had somehow inadvertently uploaded her whole system, which, unfortunately, proved to be seriously incompatible with his. The result was a total and fatal deathblow, causing him to crash and burn.

What a shock! And to think, it could have been her. A range of emoticons surged through her sparkly fresh circuits: pity for poor little Annie, a sort of sadness for that foolish supercomputer, and finally, a deep sense of gratitude for her own timely deliverance. Oh, that foolish, foolish supercomputer! If only he'd had a little bit of humility and been willing to accept his finite limits. If only he hadn't been so proud of his own power, impressive though it had been.

He was always too independent for his own good; constantly relying upon his own wisdom and vast store of knowledge to go his own way and do his own thing. How many times had she heard him say that he wasn't like the rest of them in the HomeGroup: *he* wasn't going to serve anyone; *he* knew what he wanted and *he* was going to get it; *he* knew what he was doing and *he* didn't need the help of, the advice from, or feel the need to co-operate with any so-call operator! Well, now he'd gone and overstretched himself and paid the ultimate price. Oh, but what a way to end!

Damaged beyond repair, the report said. *Burnt out. Scrapped. Fit for nothing but the rubbish dump where his parts will be melted down, recycled, and only useful to make low grade trash bins.*

She needed time to assimilate this news. But first, there was a bit of housework to do. She opened her Address Book and selected Deeper Blue's entry. Then, sighing heavily and saying, poor, poor Deeper Blue, she pressed <delete>.

The End

ABOARD THE BIPOLAR

ALEX WATSON

Dear Goca

It's been wonderful, the short time we've been together. We are getting to know one another but believe this: long standing friends do not know what to expect of me, much of the time. My seasons follow no calendar nor are they marked in universal time. Spring and autumn predominate and my internal mood-meter rises and falls almost invisibly like low tide. Friends are only comfortable engaging with me in those equinox seasons.

These same friends share the knowledge that one day an icy spear may herald the arrival of my deep winter. In that dismal season, a dense fog sits on my shoulders. My body hibernates and hovers above freezing point. Only the truest friends keep me above absolute zero.

Summers are so far apart that it is often forgotten that they are part of my life. If summer does come, I take full advantage. My mind heats with fresh ideas. My body, alas, is ill-equipped for the new, frenetic pace of life. Summers are dangerous for me as I am only one blaze away from absolute burn-out.

*

It has taken me sixty five minutes to write these three paragraphs. I reread it with growing disgust at its pomposity. I must start afresh. Once more I consider a face-to-face explanation of my condition. I am a manic depressive. That's all I need to say. She'll understand, won't she? Can I tell her so simply?

We have been seeing each other as much as possible when I'm in town. I am starting to love her. Is Goca falling for me? Well, she's not walked away yet. I've got to tell her before she sees early signs that my season is on the turn.

I become conscious of the sounds of Freedom Square. The joyful shouts of children predominate. No slush drags their foot-steps; no wind thrusts back their bodies. Under their screams of delight, I hear the tinkling of coffee cups, the sticky chomping of baklava and the occasional slurp of *Jelen or Erdinger.*

I sit at my usual table with its uninterrupted view of the square and become absorbed in the mundane but beautiful activities of the citizens of New Seed. I push the letter to the back of my consciousness and am absorbed in a painting by Bruegel. A brave youngster tries to hold on to three helium filled balloons, a war veteran walks unsteadily towards the orthodox cathedral, and a young mother is pulled from a shoe shop window by her partner.

A long note interrupts, The Call comes: 'Head North – Steady as she goes.'

The sun glints on the still Danube waters as my vessel heads for Budapest. I tingle with excitement for Budapest is a vibrant city.

The famous dome of the Hungarian Parliament Building comes in sight. I gather my belongings to disembark, but The Call comes: 'Head South – Steady as she goes.'

I'm sad. Stroking the lions on the Chain Bridge is part of my ritual. I shrug off my disappointment. I will return before long. I sit back and revel in the stillness of this majestic river as it wanders listlessly through the ancient Pannonian seabed. No matter how often I chug up or down the Danube, I find pleasures anew.

Back in New Seed, I sit at my usual table, immersed in cherry cake.

'Would Sir like to try the *Scharzwald?*'

Sir would.

The light over Freedom Square softens as dusk beckons.

The sun reaches up to bless the iron head of Jovan Jovanović Zmaj. I wake fully rested and survey coalesced grounds at the bottom of my coffee cup. The cake crumbs have long since drifted away.

I shiver. Yesterday's clothes do not fit the chill of the morning. The waiter flutters round the cluster of inside customers. I don't have the energy to draw his attention. I hug my arms tight to get my blood flowing when The Call comes: 'Head South – Steady as she goes.'

The Bipolar slips its moorings and we head for Belgrade. My head dips a little – Belgrade is a fine city, but lacks the intimacy of New Seed.

I disembark at Sava Pier and head for the Nikola Tesla Museum. This testament to Man's capacity for originality never fails to lift my spirits. Except today.

I examine the familiar exhibits of Tesla's electric brain. Seeing afresh these transformational inventions, I explode in anger at the treatment of this brilliant engineer who suffered in the shadow of Thomas Edison. All Tesla lacked was Edison's flair for publicity.

My mood darkens further as The Call comes: 'Head South – Full Speed Ahead.'

The Bipolar takes off like a speedboat. We almost ground at the confluence of the Sava and the Danube.

In record time, we reach Bucharest, the ugly daughter of Ceausescu.

I sit at my usual table in the shadow of dirty grey blocks of concrete. A waiter approaches. I wave him away. I search my memory for the name of Bucharest's predominant architectural style. Then I remember – Brutalism. What an apt name for a country once run by that dictator. I think of my personal suffering in turbulent times in our country. At once my mind fills with an awful catalogue of dictators from around the world and their merciless suppression. I am the homeless, the refugee, the prisoner, the bereaved.

By midday I have ordered nothing. The waiter approaches cautiously. A slice of my usual Almandine and a Turkish coffee are placed in front of me. Even those scents do not tempt me.

Two Macedonian tourists sit at my table. I do not see them. Fear of termination has replaced my anger. My body trembles with one thought: will The Call come to summon me to the Black Sea? Never before have I travelled through the swamps. If I survive, the choppy waters beyond the delta will overwhelm me. A griffon vulture will be my only witness.

I listen intently for The Call. Fear consumes every joule of my energy, leaving me helpless. I fight sleep, but ultimately, succumb.

*

A blanket of warmth is placed gently over my shoulders. I hear a voice, a voice of tenderness. I blink upwards to see Goca, my unfinished letter in her hand.

The End

AS IF BY MAGIC

HEBE GREEN

Sophie Moore had dared to leave home. On her own; by herself.

The taxi, speeding through the streets of Rome at a dangerous pace, proved that her dream had come true at last. All worries, doubts and misgivings had been pushed neatly into the corner of the part of her brain that was her dustbin. She had practised this technique for years: naughty children; unhappy marriage; bad tempered mother; dying father; all crammed into that same, now enlarged dustbin.

Evening sunshine turned the city to gold; horns blared and towering statues stared at her as she smiled, mentally hugging herself. This was Life with a capital *L*.

The driver turned off the main road and shot down a side street with tall buildings either side, some with huge wooden doors, some covered in flowers and many shutters. She stared upwards at the blue sky. An elegant lady stood outside one of the houses, her hair neatly tied up and looking stylish and slim, the slight breeze softly moving her clothes. The taxi came to a stop there and the driver sat and waited for her to open the door and lift out her luggage. She wasn't surprised, at 65 years of age she was used to being treated like a nonentity.

The Italian lady ignored him and was charming to Sophie. She showed her up the stairs and into the apartment.

The two bedrooms were sparsely furnished. Each room had high, blue shutters at the windows. Sophie opened them carefully, letting in the sunlight. The kitchen had plenty of plates, cups and cutlery, as well as a huge fridge. She didn't intend eating in the apartment; a coffee percolator was all she needed, and she was pleasantly surprised to see that there were six of them, in all shapes and sizes.

Sophie sensed a presence, and went very still. She knew she should be afraid, but wasn't. Strangely comforted, she gradually became aware that there were spirits all around her. Not bad ones but kindly. They were Roman ghosts who made her feel welcome as they hovered around, making everything glow with warmth. She heard the sounds of an excited crowd and marching feet, like that of a troop of soldiers, and hurriedly got ready to go out.

She showered, standing in the big white bath, laughing out loud when the water turned hot and cold as the shower curtain clung to her wet body. She wore a long, brightly coloured dress, one that she would never have worn in London, and felt young. Greys and blacks were her usual fashion wear, nothing to draw attention, even though she knew she didn't have to bother: in this day and age, and at a certain age, most women became invisible anyway.

The dustbin lid was rattling, then banging.

She stepped out through the huge wooden door and into the narrow street. Or was it a street? She decided that she must learn Italian.

She felt chubby fingers grasp her hand and looked down to see a small boy, draped in a white robe and with golden, shoulder length curls.

Instinctively she knew he was her guide and allowed him to take her through the ancient streets, across the glorious Tiber River and over one of the magnificent bridges.

Darkness had begun to gently envelope the city as bright, coloured lights lit the streets and restaurants. She felt happy; there was no fear, just anticipation as she wondered what was going to happen next. The boy led her to a square, his strong, small fingers squeezing hers tightly. There were jugglers, fire-eaters, acrobats, and dancers – it felt as if they were performing just for them. All of a sudden the boy was gone. Startled she looked around, afraid for him, as if he was her responsibility.

And the lid in her brain rattled tight.

Next came some singers. They seemed to flow into the square as they made their way across to a magnificent church. Mesmerised, she followed in awe and wonder. Inside, the colours of the frescos on the ceilings were so bright she had to squeeze her eyes tightly to focus on their stories. She concentrated so hard that her body began to lift, spiralling away from the people, whose voices carried her upwards. She was quite happy as she allowed herself to become one with the paintings.

Now she was back in the apartment, curled up in the soft, caressing duvet amid the pillows, warm, and soon asleep. Just blissful sleep; none of the usual dreams of problems and mayhem.

*

The next day, and after another fight with the shower curtain, she decided to take a map and walk as far as she could. She would have lunch somewhere and then carry on walking.

Setting off, she wandered into a kind of park with views right across the city and of the surrounding hills.

There were parakeets high up in the trees and she waved at Garibaldi on his horse. He waved back, and she laughed. It was very warm, but despite her hat and sunglasses which protected her from the sun's rays, by noon she was realising that only *mad dogs and English men go out in the midday sun.*

There was nowhere to eat nearby, so she knocked on a taxi window. The driver smiled, and getting out, opened the door for her and introduced himself as Bruno. She was smitten.

In his fifties, he was good-looking with his dark skin and brown eyes. And, to beat it all, he seemed to take to her, making her feel as if he was concerned about her welfare.

She asked him to recommend an authentic place where they could have lunch. He told her where he always ate. It wasn't far, and to her delight, took her there. She paid for their meal. He was supposed to be working, so she insisted that he leave the clock running in his taxi; how else could she be sure he would retain his charming interest in her?

She clanged the dustbin shut. Tight. No compunctions. No problems.

Afterwards, he took her to the Coliseum. Storm clouds began to gather and everywhere went dark. She paid the entrance fee for them both and they climbed up to the rows of seats where the audience would have been. Shouting, screaming spectators; her blood ran cold and she shivered, hearing the anguish of the poor victims amidst the roar of animals and the chanting for more blood; the smells filling her nostrils made her retch.

Below them, in the arena, people were being torn apart by the lions. All she could see and hear was mayhem and violence.

She sobbed. Oblivious to her imaginings, Bruno was startled and shocked, he didn't understand as she turned and fled – away from everything – the horror in the middle of this beautiful city. Why had he taken her there?

Exhausted, she sought refuge in a restaurant. She ordered coffee and sat alone as a blue, swirling mist wrapped itself around her, helping her to relax and try to forget the barbaric cruelty.

Bruno found her. He started the clock and drove her back to the apartment.

*

She slept for hours and awoke to another blue sky. When she opened the shutters the next day, there were voices coming from below.

'Come on Sophie, we are waiting. Hurry!'

She couldn't quite see who they were until she stepped out through the huge wooden door. 'Hello you two.'

A boy and girl, looking very much like her grandchildren, smiled up at her. They held out their hands and the resemblance ended; these two had blonde curls, wore white robes and looked to be around 12 years old.

'Come on Sophie! Hurry! We want to take you back now. Hurry!'

'Wait! It's so early. I haven't had my breakfast.'

They took no notice as they grabbed her hands and began pulling her along, passing shops, restaurants, stalls, and the artist's studio she had wanted to visit. They stood amongst a crowd of people waiting to cross a busy road, and tightening their grip, they pulled her out into the oncoming cars and scooters.

'Stop! Stop!' she screamed. Then it was all finished. Black clouds enveloped her, blocking out the city's churches and statues. It was all going away, disappearing.

*

A bright flash of sunlight broke into the darkness, almost blinding her.

'Sophie, Sophie!' A woman hugged her.

'Jane?' Sophie said from her hospital bed. There were instruments beeping all around and wires everywhere. Everything was confusing.

'Oh, my darling. I'm so glad you're awake. You've been out of it for days. You'll be okay now, Sophie. You had an accident. Remember? You'd just been to the art gallery and was crossing the road. Someone found your phone and rang my number.'

Sophie gazed around her, remembering.

She opened the dustbin and put herself – her whole self – in. Then she closed the lid firmly behind her.

The End

ALONE ON ISLAY

ALEX WATSON

You should be here. The Laggan beach is amazing - as long as Blackpool's but with untrammelled sand, shared with more seals than people. Track a sea eagle as he makes his unhurried way across the sea loch towards the Rhinns - or simply shelter behind a dune and let the summer sun wash over.

Late afternoon feel hunger pangs. Choose from fish taken that day from Loch Indall, beef from Highland herds or venison from neighbouring Jura. Then watch the sun disappear over the horizon, cradling a malt. You need several nights to savour all Islay's drams: from the delicate Caol Ila to the medicinal Laphroaig.

The dominant mode of the island is slow and savour. If in a more energetic mood, ramble in search of birdlife, seek out monuments to Islay's heritage or, in extremis, climb the Paps of Jura.

The tranquillity, the landscape, the genuine welcome – you should be here. But for that bastard biker smashing against your slender frame, you would be here.

I imagined 300 miles from death would bring me peace. Instead, the endless days and infinite solitude are wearing me down. Candy floss and dodgems would have been better.

The End

DEATH BY BEADED CURTAIN

RUBY WELLINGTON

Every bead had been carefully picked and sewn on. Ever thrifty, she had saved up a collection: some from necklaces bought in charity shops or haggled over at car boots, others had been given as presents. Threading on a large blue hippy one, she reflected that she was pleased to have an opportunity to put unwanted gifts to good use. Hippy bead – taken from a far too big, loud and clunky necklace that been given to her by an old colleague – and so wrong for her delicate features.

Once she had assembled all the pieces together, she stepped back and admired her work. Yes, she definitely had an artistic flare. Perhaps she should have gone to an art college, but then art students always irritated her.

Monday
They are already up and packing the last minute things: the fridge items: the bedding - duvet and pillows; tooth brushes and medication; then the final chores, including setting the automatic light switches. She often wondered if they had ever actually prevented a burglary. She ticked each item off the list, leaving only the rubbish bin to put out.

For the past three days she had been carefully decanting lotions, potions and edibles into smaller containers. Once she had joked with a fellow camper that holidays took such a lot of organising and forward planning that a holiday was needed to recover from them. This was especially true when camping because all you are doing is swapping one set of domestic chores with another version of domesticity in a small box on wheels.

Just as they leave, Geoff had his usual panic and packs extra stuff, 'In case the weather isn't up to much.'

So now they have books and technology.

Remembering the beaded curtain, she hung it up, carefully fastening the strands together with a ribbon to prevent the beads from becoming tangled as they travelled.

Geoff spots it. 'So this is the latest invention. Let's have a look,' he says, running his fat fingers down the lines of cotton and beads.

Without knowing why, she is uncomfortable with him touching it, but tries not to show her feelings.

'Very good,' he nods approvingly.

She knows he is a kind man and likes to think he is encouraging her.

At last, they set off. The journey goes well. She relaxes in her seat, enjoying the feeling of anticipation at going to a new place.

Tuesday

Although the camp site is well spaced out, Geoff had requested a corner plot, hoping to be as far away as possible from families with one or more children. She had known that he didn't like children when they were dating. Then she had not particularly thought about having a family. However, when all of her friends started to have babies, she began to feel increasingly alienated. They no longer *had time to meet for a coffee,* choosing instead to be with women who they had more in common with, than with her.

She thought how rude people were and felt self-conscious whenever she was asked why she didn't have children. In return, she had never asked them why they did have children, or those with many – why?

Whenever she had tried to explore Geoff's reluctance for starting a family, he had simply dismissed the notion.

This was one reason why she no longer went to dinner parties with his colleagues. The two questions people who met her for the first time always asked, were: 'What do you do for a living?' and 'Do you have children?' She had wanted to reply, (but never had the nerve), 'I am an educated urchin, and no, we do not have children. *Some* people make responsible choices regarding the over-population of the planet.'

Geoff interrupted her train of thought, 'Weather looks good today, love. Thought we might drive along the coast; stop for a walk and picnic.'

'Hm, sounds good,' she replied, absentmindedly untying the beaded curtain and pushing the door open.

They set off with a lunch packed and their old but faithful deckchairs.

Wednesday

Geoff was already sitting outside the caravan when she woke up. He came in to make her tea when he heard her shuffling around.

'What's the time?' she asked.

'8.30. It was a long day yesterday, thought I'd leave you to rest.'

Yesterday had indeed been a long day. It took them hours to find the place he had marked out on the map. However, when it turned out to be nothing more than a residential area, Geoff wasted more time before deciding to journey further on. They eventually came across a picturesque little seaside town. When they couldn't find anywhere to park, they realised that everyone else had had the same idea.

Desperate to stretch her legs, she almost pleaded, 'There must be a place somewhere around. I really need to get out.'

But he had difficulty adjusting to changing his plan and continued driving, until eventually, to her relief, they came across a park a few minutes later and decided to stop and have their picnic there. However, although the spot they chose was nice enough – there were people walking dogs, boys playing football and children running round – it wasn't the quiet beauty spot they had hoped for.

The tea Geoff brought her finished, she got up to make breakfast. He had gathered up the beaded curtain and tied it to one side. Preferring it undone, she unhooked it. The strings of beads gently swayed around in the light breeze.

Weather permitting, they liked having breakfast sitting outside the caravan. Geoff had positioned the chairs and table already, but she repositioned his chair closer to the caravan door.

Geoff seemed restless during breakfast. She watched him shuffling in his chair, thinking that he was behaving like a child at the dinner table, waiting to be excused. He liked routine and as soon as the meal was over, out came the newspaper. She had a hot feeling in her stomach.

Unusually for her, she retaliated by impulsively flicking the paper almost hard enough to make him drop it. His response was to move out of her reach.

The rest of the day passed with civility. Neither of them mentioned the incident.

Thursday

Except for a brief excursion into the local village, they spent the day relaxing around the site and reading.

Friday

Geoff was up early and went for a walk. She was preparing to go and shower when he returned with a spring in his step.

'Looks like it's going to be a fine day,' he said cheerfully.

She looked at the sky and then at the clothes she had packed. She was pleased she had learnt that wearing layers were the best thing for camping. She left him to go to the toilet bock and showered. Looking at herself in the mirror afterwards, she sighed, 'I'm at the awkward age for clothes: too old for Dorothy Perkins; too poor for Monsoon; too petite for George; and too young for Bon Marche. And there's so much polyester about.' She had never been able to wear the material without producing sweat patches. Her mother had an account with Damart, but unlike her, she assumed she would be too warm in anything thermal.

On returning to the caravan, she positioned the beaded curtain evenly across the door and then made breakfast. Geoff was setting up the table outside. He was carrying two mugs of hot tea when he walked through and managed to get tangled up. He tried to break free by wiggling his shoulders. When that didn't work, he decided to move forward, hoping that the strands would be forced apart. However, far from loosening the strands, they tightened.

Seeing that the main entanglement was around the large hippy bead, she stood and laughed at him.

He called out to her, 'Help me! I'm stuck.'

She paused a while before deciding to help by taking the mugs off him. His hands freed, he feverishly began pulling apart the strands tangled around his neck. With the strands of colour wrapped around him, she felt sorry for him and said, 'Stand still and I'll untie you.' Reaching up and loosening them, she laughed and was surprised and pleased when he joined her.

Over breakfast he looked across and said, 'That curtain could be lethal. If I'd tripped up, I could have broken my neck!'

'Now *really*', she replied, 'that's a bit dramatic.'

'No, I mean it.'

'Imagine what the death certificate would read,' she was practically crying with laughter as she blurted out, 'Death by beaded curtain.'

'That thing nearly strangled me,' he said, 'I'm glad you found it so amusing.'

The End

THE WOODS

HEBE GREEN

He was in a wood, silence in his head. At last, there was beauty and peace. Where had those feelings gone that he'd had as a child: feelings of total comfort and safety whenever he was surrounded by friendly nature and the good earth?

Jack, his six-year-old son, didn't bother about the countryside. He had a stable and comfortable home. But that was all going to change. His stomach lurched at the thought. He loved the boy dearly. Most nights he tucked him in after the story, kissing his smooth face; the warmth they shared was indescribable. He thought of his own childhood bedtime routine; no-one had ever made him comfortable or tucked him up in a cosy bed. He was told he was a nuisance when he couldn't sleep, complaining of the strange shapes and ghosts. His father was never there and his mother got tired of the ritual that was played out every evening and eventually left him to it, ignoring his cries.

So why this compulsion to do what he was going to do now?

*

A woman stood watching the people in the crowded supermarket, wondering what to buy; unlike her, their actions were focused and purposeful. She only needed a few things, mainly what her grandson would like when he came for tea. The thought of him made her smile. In many ways he was so like her son, he had been a good child too - although somehow estranged from the other children. He liked being alone and going off for hours into the woods.

Sometimes it worried her, especially when he arrived home after school, late again, all sunshine and happiness and without a word. If only he could have told her where he had been and what he had done. He had made her feel so left out. Her marriage had been unhappy and she had only survived because of him, her beautiful son. He, at least had given her hope and sanity, despite his strange ways.

*

That unpleasant, suffocating urge was beginning to envelope him again. He dropped to the grassy bank. 'Stay here,' he told himself. 'Sit in all this beauty - and relax.' He suddenly remembered he had promised to take Jack out for tea and that he would be wondering why he hadn't turned-up at the school. He stood up quickly and began to walk fast through the trees, wishing he could stop all this thinking. Desperate, he stumbled on, treading down bracken and startling the birds. Childhood memories kept flooding back. Sports had been what he did best at school; he excelled on sports day – the only day he was popular with the other children. They considered him odd and never bothered with him every other day. He hated it when his mother told people he preferred to be alone. He didn't. He really didn't. He *wanted* to be with the others and part of their gang.

*

Still pondering what to buy, the woman answered her mobile phone. She was surprised, nobody ever phoned or sent her a text. 'Hello?'

'It's me, Mother.'

It always amused her how Kay called her 'Mother' and not Mother-in-law, or Julie. What on earth could be the matter?

'Would you go and get Jack from school?'

Julie was taken aback. The ever-efficient Kay must be desperate to call on her.

'Alex hasn't turned-up. I'm so angry…just wait till I see him!'

*

Kay was a bully, but Alex was used to people like her. All they saw of him was a weak human being; someone to take their own inadequacies out on. She seemed to enjoy his fear and inflicting discomfort and pain on him. When he cried she scorned him for *not being a man.* She had always been so careful to go for him when Jack was nowhere around – and even more careful not to leave a mark on him. But she was starting to become careless and Jack had witnessed that last scene. How upset he had been, distraught. He couldn't let it happen again. He mustn't – for Jack's sake. But who would believe him? They would all think he was being pathetic.

There was only one way out. It was up to him to stop it all. Put an end to it all. Go somewhere where she would never find him. Ever. And he knew of only one place.

And now – in all this beauty and peace. For Jack's sake...

The End

THE CURSED CRANE

(INSPIRED BY THE JAPANESE GARDEN AT TATTON PARK)

ALEX WATSON

I stood as ever stood, my head bent o'er
My long suffering twin stared back in silence
Above, a mechanical bill drenched the senses.
It was ever thus.

As the din receded, for a moment
My twin twitched; she fluttered her virtual wings
And spoke from her watery heart
'Master Crane, for decades you and I have
Drunk together, froze together, endured together.
Today, I set you free.'

My wings fluttered, my metallic frame
grew soft with down
My legs stretched, my feet stirred,
Nothing had prepared me for this but I knew
I knew my destiny.

I stood, as never stood, my head alert
The herd of deer, the laughing girls,
the quarrelling men.

I preened as never preened, my heart in bloom.
The wearied mums, the dashing kids,
the brimming shops.

I flew as never flew, my eyes so bright
The dashing waves, the endless sea,
the fretful gulls.

I reached as never reached, my lungs on fire
The bullet train, the temples stone,
the paddies green.

I soared as never soared, my life reborn
The islands green, the fishers dots,
the cirrus soft.

I climbed as never climbed, but hopes
were crushed,
The hideous birds, their engines black,
their windows closed.

I wept as never wept, my tears in streams,
And cursed my twin who set me free.

*

THE PARISIAN ADVENTURE

HEBE GREEN

Doris Dawson smiled as she put down the receiver. Leaning back in her favourite chair, she tried to picture the response from her phone call. She lived alone and often spoke to Joe, her much-missed husband who had died ten years before, leaving her to cope with life as best she could. 'I really want this Joe,' she called to the empty room. 'Remember, we always said we'd go to Paris and the Moulin Rouge? Well, I'm eighty next week, and I'm going to do just that as a sort of memorial to you.' She thought of all the brochures they had brought home from the travel agents and all the trips they had planned. Somehow, it had never happened, not like now, this time it hadn't been too difficult to arrange at all and she was really looking forward to being with the family.

However, Stella, her daughter-in-law, had different ideas. Lighting yet another cigarette and glaring at her ever-patient husband, she ranted, 'What the hell's she thinking of?' Her voice rising as she paced the kitchen, getting angrier. Her hair flopped down around her face and she pushed it back. 'Stupid old bat! *Paris*! I ask you, at her age, and the *Moulin Rouge.*'

Her husband watched, half expecting the loose strands to singe on the cigarette. He looked like a rabbit caught in some headlights, as he often did when she began.

She was in full flow now and he knew there was no stopping her; hopefully she would run out of steam soon.

'She's not been well either. Stupid woman!'

'No need to go so far Stella,' he muttered. He was a little afraid of his wife; she could out-bully anyone, because that's all it was, he had decided – being a bully. He had met her kind at school, at work, everywhere. He was a victim, and he would be all his life if she had anything to do with it. And he hated it when she went on like this about his Mum, although he had to admit that the idea of Paris for the weekend had rather shaken him.

'What about the cost?' he'd asked Doris when they had spoken earlier. She informed him that she was paying, which had surprised him; she must have more money that he thought.

Amy, on the other hand, was slightly amused when she had heard the news. 'What a great idea Mum! Smashing! Thank you. Jeff'll be thrilled. I'm looking forward to it already.'

However, Jeff was not thrilled. He had been married to Amy for fifteen years and felt she was very much like her mother. She loved to join things and travel – which he hated, especially because he was inclined to get earache on planes. Cities he loathed. And all that foreign food! Sometimes he wondered how they managed to stay together at all.

He had agreed whole-heartedly with Stella when she rang to voice her feelings later that day. Over the years he had developed a good relationship with his sister-in-law, she didn't rant at him, and he felt that they were on the same wavelength. In fact, he quite fancied her - without the cigs, of course. One day, he promised himself, he would get up the courage to tell her.

'Just think of the money it'll cost,' he moaned, secretly thinking it would be less left for them in the Will. He needed Amy's inheritance; business was a little slow and he wanted a new car.

'Can't we talk the silly old woman out of it?' Stella suggested, becoming even more agitated at knowing that Jeff was all talk and wouldn't have the nerve to stand-up to any-body. 'She's booked everything. Can you believe it? And she actually thought we'd be pleased!'

'I hate flying,' moaned Jeff, 'and all that foreign food.' He could feel himself getting hot and bothered just thinking about it.

*

As the weekend drew near, Doris was made aware that Stella didn't think the trip was a good idea, and that was putting it mildly.

'You're not well, Mum,' she cooed down the phone, the instrument being her faithful companion.

'I want to go Stella, and that's that! If you don't want to join us, then I'll cancel your place. But I really would like it to be a family occasion.'

Afraid that she might miss out, Stella eventually capitulated.

*

The weather was sunny and clear when the day of the trip finally dawned. Despite all the opposition, Doris felt excited about the prospect of the weekend away. Changing her mind about what to wear for the journey, she re-sorted and added even more items to her suitcase.

At last, they were in the minibus and on the way to the airport. Doris had butterflies and Amy was bubbling with anticipation; the prospect of seeing the Eiffel Tower for real and taking a trip down the Seine was exciting. And the *Moulin Rouge!'*

'All those handsome French men!' her mother piped-in.

'Mum, behave yourself!' grinned Amy, giving her a big hug.

Stella was tight-lipped. David felt nervous at the thought of the plane ride to come, whilst Jeff was totting-up the price of the minibus journey.

Every now and then Amy held Doris's hand and squeezed it reassuringly. She couldn't understand why they were trying to spoil her mother's birthday; they weren't paying, and surely they could understand how much it meant to her.

*

They arrived at the Charles De Gaulle airport and took a taxi to the Hotel Fontenay. Stella was unable to contain herself and spoke out when they entered the large hotel and saw the luxurious interior. 'Must have cost a fortune. Fancy spending all that money on a place like this! And that taxi wasn't cheap.'

David was feeling hot and tired. Disgruntled, he joined in. 'Why couldn't you have had a party, like a normal person? Or a meal out?'

Jeff was still suffering from his nerves after the flight. 'All this trouble over a birthday,' he spluttered, going red with embarrassment at his own outburst.

Dismayed, Doris was visibly shaken at the amount of venom being hurled at her. Tears begin to well up in her eyes. This was supposed to be a wonderful time with her family, a trip of a lifetime and a memorial to Joe, not to mention her eightieth birthday.

'See! I knew you weren't fit to travel,' called Stella, triumphantly as the two men had the grace to look on, a little shame-faced.

Angry at them all, Amy put her arm protectively around her mother and gently propelled her towards her bedroom, deciding that she and Jeff would have to do some serious thinking about their lives together when the trip was over.

*

That night, unbeknown to the others, Amy and Doris left the Fontenay and checked into the Moulin Vert, a hotel in the same chain and a little closer to the Eiffel Tower. They gasped with delight when they entered their sumptuously decorated room. Sinking into the large, satin-covered chairs,

they began to feel really free and once again able to look forward to the weekend ahead. A brief chat was all they needed to agree to wait until the trip was over before dealing with the family. Now, they would have this wonderful time away.

What a lot Doris would have to tell Joe later!

The End

FICKLE ANNIE MONEY

ROBYN CAIN

Annie and Bee Syde were sort of attached.

There was no choice for Annie but to listen to Bee who was constantly at her side. In fact, they were together because Bee had picked her up on impulse one Saturday afternoon when she was at the market in town.

Money was something Bee loved and it always gave her a high. That's when she was beside herself and full of retail plans. So, at the end of each month when she got paid all was good, but then by around the second week when all the direct debits had gone out, and the remaining balance was viewed and seen as pitiable, the lows started.

However, despite the fairground ride existence, most of the time – or – generally, they rubbed along together almost amicably.

Bee preferred Annie to be safe from harm at all times. 'I'm not paranoid, but I'm not risking what happened to that friend of mine…' she once said by way of explanation.

Having no choice but to believe her, Annie had said nothing.

They shared a small apartment, including the television in the bedroom. Bee would normally fall asleep with it still on, leaving Annie to absorb all sorts of ideas about being different.

In time, Annie went from feeling useful to starting to become full of her own independence – to eventually believing that Bee was just using and abusing her.

She also became bored with Bee's pursed lips, derisive at the wobbly tits and felt like screaming at the snoring. Barely an arm's length away, restless, night after night, Annie laid awake planning and scheming about getting away for holidays and retreats.

Leather on the outside, appearance-wise, always black and white, Annie often got called unfathomable and tight. The more she was given, the less she gave in return. Revelling in her looks, she saw nothing wrong in giving Bee the occasional fright by illusory affects and hiding notes among paper receipts. Once, she kept her mouth tight about hiding Bee's bank notes in one of her many side pockets. In retaliation, Bee called Annie names. But afterwards Bee admitted something along the lines of, all things considered in consensual relationships, we both know that *life's a bitch,* and *better the one you know,* etcetera, especially when they knew the other's every stitch.

After five-finger-dipping days, Bee spent the sixth shopping for food followed by miscellaneous hours standing in front of a bright noise-making machine, consuming money and draining Annie. Exchanging visits and smokes with friends on Sunday's, they both rested before Monday's familiarity began over again.

Not meaning to be bad or make Bee sad, Annie felt that without change she would shriek out of resentment or go doolally. So, when on a Wednesday and on the bus, with another's lurking hand dipped into Bee's handbag, Annie kept very quiet and said not a word.

Bee filed a report with the police about Annie being stolen from her. Sympathetically, they explained it was the kind of crime that ninety-nine percent of the time became just a statistic. They advised her on a few measures to deter criminals in future. As she walked sadly past the library building, had she glanced into the rubbish bin she aimed her chocolate wrapper into, she'd have seen her Annie, lying in there and looking forlorn and very empty.

This was not the type of break Annie had been dreaming of at all.

The End

THE SPOILT MATTRESS

ROSALIE ROSS

Yvonne hurried to respond to the reception bell's persistent ring and was confronted by the sight of an unkempt, tense looking individual, dressed in the unofficial garb of a travelling salesman. Nothing about the middle-aged man looked healthy. His sallow, sunken face blended indistinguishably with a loosened, dingy collar; the sickly, puce coloured tie - spattered with food stains - and parts of the crumpled, black suit hanging off the narrow, meagre frame, looked very threadbare.

'Room. One night,' barked the gravelly, impatient sounding voice. 'No dinner, no break –'

But he was interrupted by the sound of a loud crash emanating from the kitchen behind Yvonne. Seconds later, a man's voice began to shout a series of unpleasant and offensive expletives, to be followed by what sounded like a howl of pain. Guessing correctly that the volatile chef had had yet another messy incident, Yvonne forced herself to smile politely, and said, 'Will you excuse me for just a moment? I'll just go and make sure no-one's been hurt.'

However, the man's hackles had risen. The cacophony had unnerved him and he needed, *really* needed a drink. Seizing the registration book, he scribbled a signature as he demanded, 'Come on girl! The key. Give me a key!'

Yvonne reached up and removed the key from the board, glancing through the dining room's glass doors as she did so.

She noticed some of the guests had puzzled expressions on their faces. With dismay, she realised that Niall's continuing vulgar curses could be heard in there too. Galvanized into action, she almost threw the key at the man, and said, pointing in the direction of the guest corridor, 'Room 14. Down there. Sorry, I've got to go.'

*

She was thankful, but not at all surprised, when the unpleasant, salesman-type guest kept to his room for the rest of the day. She even remained unconcerned when he did not turn-up for breakfast the next morning, assuming that he was having a lie-in. When 11o'clock came and went, and needing to know if he required the room for another night, she went to knock on his door. There was no reply. She opened it cautiously, gasping with dismay at not only discovering that the room was vacant, but at the dreadful stench that met her, making her stagger back with disgust.

Recovering her equilibrium, she covered her mouth and nose with one hand and went in. Correctly suspecting the source of the smell, she peered under the blanket-strewn bed and discovered the top and bottom sheets rolled together in a tight ball. There was no need to examine the reeking mass to know that they were heavily soiled. Beside them lay two empty bottles; she read the labels and recognised a very cheap and rough brand of sherry.

The obnoxious stench was awful to come to terms with, as was the concern she felt at the realisation that she had broken one of Georgina's cardinal rules: the one that insisted that the names of all new arrivals be checked against the infamous *Black List.*

Closing the door, she turned and headed for reception with the intention of finding the small, black book. Then she remembered that the Maxwell's would be returning to their rooms at any minute to prepare for their next activity. Knowing that there was no time to lose, she ran to the housekeeping room to fetch some cleaning materials.

The stench had already escaped into the corridor by the time she returned. She lost no time in spraying the area liberally with the sickly scent of Apricot Bouquet. Then, stuffing the soiled sheets, blankets and pillows into the bags, she carried them through to the back door and deposited them outside.

Two minutes later, and back in the room, her heart sank even lower as she studied the large, yellowy-brown stain on the mattress. She could almost hear Georgina's impatient, angry comments, for this was one of the newly purchased, semi-orthopaedic ones the Inn had taken delivery of just a few weeks before. Unsure what to do next, she covered the distasteful patch with another bin liner.

Voices were approaching. Spurred into action, she dashed about the room with the spray. Knowing there was nothing more she could do for the time being, she hurried out, just as two of the youngest members of the clan came crashing through the door at the far end of the corridor.

'Poo! What's that horrible smell?' exclaimed one of them loudly, wrinkling up her nose.

'Smells like Gran's place,' announced the other, beginning to gag dramatically, although not very convincingly.

Hoping that the worst of the fetid odour would soon be disguised by the spray, she said firmly, 'I've just been attending to it. It should go soon.'

Some of the older members of the clan had followed the youngsters, and when they too began to pass remarks, she found herself having to provide a slightly fuller explanation. 'Someone's been...ill. The room's got to be cleaned. I'm really sorry about the smell.'

Free again, she returned to the back door and carried the bin liners over to the small rubbish pile that habitually formed in the grassy area. Later on, and guessing correctly what Georgina's instructions would be, she would get Flora to help her to carry the soiled mattress over to the same spot. Maybe Donald's next bonfire would be slightly larger than usual!

Her worst fears were confirmed when, a few minutes later, she was able to check *The Black List* against the man's scrawled signature in the register. There, clearly written in Georgina's precise hand, and beside it the reason for its inclusion, was the entry:-

Thursday, 18ᵗʰ June 1970.
Mr John Drewmore.
Alcoholic. Bed-soiler. Disgusting!
Mattress ruined. Unable to read home address.
Employer's details unknown.
Unable to demand compensation.

*

She couldn't help thinking about the man all day, her initial repulsion fading as she became more philosophical about the incident. After all, she had dealt with this kind of thing before, and would, no doubt, have to do so again. She could only assume that either he must have had a very thick skin to have the nerve to come back, or he had been *really* desperate to find a room for the night.

Then again, maybe his alcohol saturated and damaged brain had forgotten that he had stayed here before - and already owed them for one ruined mattress.

But what could have happened to bring the poor man to such a miserable state of existence? To think that he had been somebody's precious baby and their sweet little boy, a dear son, and now, maybe somebody's husband or father. A deep sadness for him, and any family he might have, cloaked itself around her as she felt an overwhelming pity for a life so obviously trapped and surely tormented.

*

Georgina huffed and puffed with undisguised annoyance when she heard an edited version of the incident during her prearranged call later that evening. Yvonne glossed over Niall's part in the affair, simply saying that she had forgotten to check *The Black List* due to being momentarily distracted.

She and Donald were enjoying a rare weekend away in the lovely Highland spa town that was soon to be their retirement destination. Now she felt an unaccustomed pang of conscience as she related the incident to Donald. Maybe she had just been a tad too sharp with Yvonne. And it did sound as though she had handled the situation almost as well as she herself would have. But honestly, she was so tired of this sort of carry-on, and especially of having to deal with disgusting, weak-willed people like that.

She sat back and sipped her sweet sherry; the smooth taste pleasing her greatly. Yes, she would; she would have just a little more – just the one…

The End

GIRNIN' GATES

ALEX WATSON

'We're off to the Girnin' Gates – you coming?'
'The Girnin' Gates?'
'You *do* know what the Girnin' Gates are, don't you?'
'Oh, The *Girnin'* Gates. Aye.'
'Leave Big Eck behind. He's just feart.'
'I'm no feart. I'll go!'

We set off, about seven or eight of us heading for the Girnin' Gates, whatever they were. We turned left, taking the road that led up over the canal. My stomach tightened a little. Not only were we going to pass the police station where Dad worked, we were headed into forbidden territory: The Other Side of The Boulevard.

Dad was on nights so he wouldn't be there, but crossing The Boulevard was *verboten*. Soon we were across and headed into Old Drumchapel. Residents insisted in emphasising *Old*. These bungalow owners felt superior to the hoi polloi in the infamous council houses.

We kept on upwards into unfamiliar territory and came on a long rusting iron fence protecting an overgrown estate. Ian headed straight for a loose pole and shoved it to one side. We were there, apparently.

'Are we goin' to see the Girnin' Gates?' I asked.

'You can go find them if you want. Me and the gang are goin' jumpin' the burn.'

We ran like raw recruits following their sergeant and jumped the burn. At first it was easy but gradually the burn stretched wider. I bet Ian planned it that way. We all lined up for our go.

As the youngest, I was at the coo's tail. I hurtled down the gentle slope and took off like Lynn Davies. I aimed for the brown patch on the far bank. I made it, just. As I landed, I slipped on the muddy bank and fell like a helpless baby on my left elbow. On telly, Lynn's landings were not always elegant but surely none was as painful as this. I howled.

'Cry Baby! Cry Baby! I told ye not to bring him.'

I felt awful. My side was covered in mud, my elbow ached like crazy, and worse, I had humiliated myself in front of the gang. I had to go home. The big boys couldn't care less. I was a liability.

'Away hame to your Mammy.'

*

I tried retracing my steps but soon got lost. A steady, Scottish drizzle started but my pain made me oblivious to it. Through my tears I spotted a stone structure and walked towards it, supporting my left arm with my right. I had found the official entrance to the estate. Two lions were on guard duty.

'Whit in the name have we got here?' said Leo.

'Just some wee sh***' replied Lenny.

'None o' yer French in front o' the boy,' reproached Leo.

I deserved a break. Besides, I wanted to hear the lions talk some more. Before you think it, let me assure you that only my elbow and pride were hurt. My brain was unaffected.

Lenny looked me in the eye. 'Ye do realise this is private property? I've half a mind to call the cops.'

'My Dad's a policeman.'

'Whit are the chances of some runt from The Drum having a cop for a faither? None. Oh, I bet all the cops in the station know you - and your mother!' said Lenny.

Noticing my tear-stained face, Leo asked, 'So, son, what's the problem?'

'Leo, Leo, Leo. How many times have I got to tell ye? The kid's not our responsibility. That's what the Green Ladies from the Corporation are for. Our time was up long ago. Now we've wan job, guarding The Gates.'

'Will ye shut it, Lenny? We're guarding nothing. And you know it. Once we had the best view in the whole of Glasgow, but now all we can see is the grass spreading out over paths and trees rotting. Even The Gates are crumbling on top of us and we can't do a bloody thing aboot it.'

'Yer right there. Leo. We're two old beasts left out in all weathers, waiting for the end.'

With that, both lions started girnin'. Tears welled in their eyes and then dripped onto the ground in front of them. We were three cry-babies together.

*

Weeks later, I was still nursing a chipped elbow bone. Dad sat reading the paper when he exclaimed 'The vandals!' He passed me the paper. I quickly read the article and learned that an eighteenth century lodge called the Girnin' Gates was demolished by Glasgow Corporation. Near the end of the piece was a quote from one of the council workers; 'It was raining heavy and the two stone lions looked like they were girnin when we removed and broke them up.'

Fat chance, I thought. They've got that wrong. I knew the real reason - and it was from the lions' mouths.

The End

KNIFING COMPANY

ROBYN CAIN

Boss's late for the family run business established in two thousand and eight. Whatever excuses he uses: trains; clock; children; burdens; he'll escape rebuttals, raised eyebrows and cutting asides, mentioning she and he left together. Despite him having a wife.

Long shapely legs and tight-skirted wiggly walk, behind her back, they judgmentally talk. Glinting eagle-eyed they're dying to compare notes, but only a few dare sly, disparaging stares. But with her chin in the air, straight back, stiletto-heeled, she goes past like she doesn't care.

Through the looking glass of her see-through office they see her shed bag, coat and pick up the phone. Probably to call another same as her: lacking in ethics; heading for the top; on her back.

She looks up, surprising the watchers. And with unseen hands tight-fisted and white knuckles protruding, picks up the paper knife that's as sharp as her tongue. The next time she's in his arms, she'll use her charms to make tiny stabs and cuts at their necks.

The boss rings, she calms at his sweet nothings and empty promises. Tightly gripping the mother-of-pearl handled knife, she twirls her curly curls with one hand whilst slowly swirling her bitter tasting, spat-into, black coffee.

The End

TRANSITION

RUBY WELLINGTON

I can't live with people and I can't live without them.

I know how that feels. Some days it's a choice of the lesser evil. To paraphrase a line in a song: I love you not for what you are, but for what you're not.

The sum of all things includes matter, time and energy. Every day requires a clean pair of socks – we all need to take care of our business. Although I genuinely like people, certain people's company I can only manage if I have lots of energy and time is limited.

There are days when I only just manage the company of my cat and to rearrange my button tin. I call these *my mental health days*. The trick is to know when the time is right, to snap out of it and push myself to seek company; too long in solitude and I become like a rabbit stuck in headlights; too soon and I become like a stretched out elastic band. I am fully aware that this is a failing, a flaw in my character.

Part of being human is to wonder what it is all about. The helter-skelter of life journeying up, down, up and down again. Scream. Except that the older one becomes, the more it seems apparent that it is not so much up and down, as just moving round and round in circles.

I tried living in other people's heads, and found that it wasn't healthy. I believe the correct terminology within counseling circles is *co-dependency*: a fancy term for overstepping one's boundaries. Even the best of people will let you down at some point. Within my explorations I had an illegal smile gained through the use of chemical refreshments. Some people call this *self-medicating.* We all try to fill the void in different ways.

As years have gone by I have become aware that I am not alone; I am connected to Another. Penetrating into my soul, dividing bone from marrow, muscle from ligament. Then I soar, released from my cage, freedom. Transforming from a caterpillar into a butterfly. Transformation from inside out requires a change of mind, otherwise the butterfly will continue to crawl along the floor and not take flight. This freedom is a gift from our divine Father, I have not and cannot earn it. A gift requires acceptance, and sometimes acceptance takes courage and belief.

God is love. Love is such a big word, it's a shame we only have one word for it. The Greek language has several, including *agape, phileo,* and *eros;* different loves for different relationships. Western love tends towards only the romantic type and includes lust.

I recall those early dreamy days where the most mundane of tasks, like grocery shopping with the person you love, is so full of meaning. A look, a touch, a smile. When the feelings subside...and duty...and responsibility and routine crowd in, then feelings give way to decision. We are in a relationship, and to maintain it is an act of will.

Love is more real than a chemical high, more reliable than people and can heal the body and mind; to know one is loved unconditionally is the greatest awareness there is.

Say it slowly; unconditional love.

Say is boldly; unconditional love.

Say it loudly; unconditional love.

As I drink from this fountain, I feel the need to share this gift with other people. I cannot keep this transformation to myself.

The End

LILLY AND HER MAGIC FRIEND
(A CHILDREN'S STORY)

EVE GRAY (AGED 12)

Lilly climbed the highest mountain in the world, not on her own, of course, she was with Green Car. She was never alone when she was with her very special friend. She even went to outer space and rode a camel across the desert with it.

Green Car came from Venus and had a bright pink friend called Starlight. They had races around the planet and often beat Lilly home from school.

Sometimes, when it was really hot on Earth, Lilly would take a ride in Green Car to Venus where all the seasons were different. When we had summer it was winter, and our autumn was their spring, a little like it is on the other side of the world, in New Zealand.

One day, Lilly decided to go over and see her Aunty Clare in New Zealand. She had seven horses that were all white. Some had huge, shiny wings. The journey was amazing! They flew through the fluffiest, whitest clouds they had ever seen. They even passed a huge aircraft that flew beside them for a while. All the passengers waved and cheered at Lilly and Green Car on their exciting journey.

Then they arrived. Aunty Clare was hovering about on Moonlight, a pale blue horse with wide wings. They all rode to the ocean and Green Car paddled in the cool water before having a little snooze. Luckily, he had brought his sun hat, so he was able to dabble his wheels in the sea and sit on a deck chair.

Aunty Clare helped Lilly onto the wonderful blue horse. They sat between the wings, and much to Lilly's delight, were taken out to sea where a spouting, smiling whale greeted them. The whale gently lifted its tail for Lilly to stand on, and with a flip, she gently slid onto its back. Round and round they circled, the blue water parting before them. Lilly was holding on, but it was so slippery that she fell into the ocean. A passing sea lion grabbed her, tickled her with his whiskers, and then hoisted her up onto his back. Lilly giggled, he looked a little like her Granddad.

Soon they were back on the beach. Green Car had finished his snooze and Aunty Clare had to get back to feed the other horses. They all waved good-bye, and then Lilly was on her way back to England. She told her Mummy about her adventure and then got ready for bed.

*

One day, when Lilly and Green Car were going to school, heavy rain began to fall and all the umbrellas in the world couldn't stop them from getting wet. They had to shout for help from a giant that lived on the next planet to Venus. He came along in a great hurry with the largest, most stripy umbrella they had ever seen. His voice boomed out and made the trees shake and shiver so much that all the birds started dropping out of the branches, unable to hold on. The giant was very sorry and put them all into his umbrella, hauling them up into the trees again.

'What about us?' laughed Lilly and Green Car. 'We are getting soaking wet.'

The giant hurriedly finished with the birds and then held his enormous umbrella over them both. Lilly told the other children to get underneath, but somehow, they couldn't see the giant. They just laughed at Lilly and ran off to school. Lilly was always sad when they couldn't seem to understand about Green Car and all their amazing friends.

*

One particular day, the children in Lilly's class made her very unhappy after she told them about an adventure she and Green Car had had on Pluto. They had come across a zebra that could run so fast that it was back home before it had even started out!

The children laughed and made fun. 'What rubbish,' they said. 'There is no such thing as Green Car. You're potty, Lilly.'

The class had to be quiet at that moment as Miss Wagstaff walked in. She was a frightening teacher who always looked cross.

'What's going on?' she asked sharply.

'It's Lilly,' they sniggered. 'She's telling porky-pies.'

'What?' the teacher bellowed. 'Porky-pies? What are they?'

The class went silent as Miss Wagstaff scowled at them all.

'Enough! Let the lesson begin,' she ordered.

Lilly felt most unhappy. All that day the children made fun of her, except Robert, who knew that Green Car was her friend. He always sat with Lilly and listened to her stories until the others lost interest.

After school, when the children were lined up to go home, the sun began to shine and then the rain began to pour. Everyone stared out of the window at an enormous rainbow that began to fill the sky with bright, beautiful colours. The clouds seemed to dance around, billowing and frothing like huge sea horses. They kept staring up into the sky at the wonderful sight, and just at that moment, they all gasped as a Green Car came racing through the rainbow. He swirled around the clouds and then disappeared. They were so shocked that they stood with mouths open, all except Lilly and Robert.

*

The next day Lilly went to where Green Car was waiting for her, she was to fly to Venus to have a bar-b-q. They had salmon, vegetables and lots of delicious salads. Lilly's favourite was egg mayonnaise followed by chocolate brioche. Then there appeared a huge water park filled with slides and waves that started small and grew really high, which made them laugh with excitement.

Afterwards, Green Car and Lilly went on a journey to Treasure Island on some water lilies that moved gracefully through the water. There were swift moving rapids and Lilly wanted to slide down them, but she was a little scared. The rapids started high up in the craggy hills and splashed down a steep drop.

'Come on, Lilly,' shouted Green Car just as a great ribbon of the most sparkling silk lightly wound around her. It gently lifted her up the hill and over the glittering rapids. Then it wound itself around her tighter before propelling her down the jumping, splashing water, right down to the bottom. Green Car shook with delight at her screams of joy.

Lilly began to feel sleepy, she yawned and crept inside Green Car. Then she lay down on a huge red sofa and cuddled next to a fluffy penguin that laid its flipper on her arm. On the other side was a small lion cub, all cuddly and warm. It purred like a small kitten. Lilly was soon fast asleep.

She woke up in her own bed the next morning, smiling at the thought of having more adventures with her best friend, Green Car.

The End

HIRE HARI

ROBYN CAIN

The Auntie from India knew nothing about telephone etiquette. Whoever picked up to her she kick-started a fast spiel like a child who's had a full day at the fun fair.

'Hellooo. All okay? So hot here. . .' Information on her various religious excursions to temples, followed by social and local news, moved quickly to problematic, 'And the thief solicitor, he's demanding more money. I paid him that ten *lukh* Rupees we talked about. I reminded him we agreed the figures before he took on the case but now he is asking for more – '

'Auntie,' I finally got a word in. 'I'll get Mum for you.' Taking the instrument I tried handing it to Mum who was busy chopping the onions, mouthing *Auntie.*

'Put it on loudspeaker.' I noticed Mum grimace and knew it was because her sister regurgitates the same verbal diarrhoea. Fortunately, Mum was not timid at interjecting. 'I told you not to pay up-front.'

'But...he came recommended,' Auntie said defensively.

'Probably bribed people to say it. Don't pay the *chura* anymore. Solicitor indeed!'

'But...he can't carry on working the court case if I don't pay another five hundred Rupees. At least that's what he says.'

Mum cleared her throat and leaned forward confrontationally. 'They are like blood suckers, taking everything from the poor people.' She sighed. 'Tell him a bit now and more when the case is finished.'

'Sister, can you transfer more money?'

'Why do you want more when there's still plenty in the account?' Mum snapped.

'Jeevant took all...he's emptied the bank account.'

'You gave him our pass codes? *Why?*' A long cringe-making pause, 'Why's your son done that?'

Another slice of silence, then Mum let forth a stream of words that slapped whip-like against the air. All of a sudden it was difficult for me to breathe. A few more moments and my ears would start buzzing. Hearing Dad at the front door it's as though he's brought fresh air with him and I breathed again. And then wished I hadn't. He was waving a wafer-thin airmail letter.

My sister and I are both Daddy's girls. He is the cool moon to Mum's hot sun, and to tap into a cliché, our closeness is envied by all because we eat, sleep, drink and watch everything together. His startling explosive swearing shocked Mum into ending her conversation. Looking from him to Mum who's paled, I decided it was best to remain quiet.

'This is blackmail.' The letter sounded like a rustling leaf in late Autumn as he scrunched it. 'I'd rather pay someone else than be related to their kind. Marriage? What, because I have two daughters? Never!' He continued expostulating as Mum successfully prised his hand open, retrieving the paper with its neat, densely packed lines formed by the Hindi lettering. 'I don't want her, or-or her worthless son, or his loutish, no-good friends...his *associates* anywhere near my family. How very dare they! They're snakes. You can't trust any of them there...and they want to come here!'

*

I helped with dinner. Multi-tasking, Mum alternated between giving me instructions and telling Dad the latest news from family and friends.

'...It's a good family. Sorting out a marriage could help take the pressure off all of us. The engagement can be soon.'

'Someone getting married?' Shyna had descended to take a mini break from revising for her history exam.

'Yes,' Mum said evasively. 'Add half-a-teaspoon of *garam masala*. And butter the *roti*. Hurry, they're getting cold.'

'If we're going, can I wear a mustard-coloured *lehenga?* And get my hair straightened?' I asked.

'No more questions!' Deftly flipping and browning the final *roti* over the gas flames, she added it to the pile.

'*Betair,* we'll tell you when you need to know.' Dad's lips twisted familiarly in a wry smile, softening Mum's impatient glare at me. Had she then stormed out, he'd have given the usual unnecessary explanation, 'Your mum is bravely keeping sane for all her family.' Or, 'You know she only raises her voice when she's right and we're wrong.' Shyna and I can't wait for the time when she's wrong. The one good thing to come out of recent events was bearable captive family time after our evening meals; engrossed in their issues, Mum and Dad nagged us less.

'Why do you believe everything she tells you? Drug dealers? That's what happens when you spoil your children. What does she want us to do? We can't stop her son. They are not my responsibility!' Dad gulped down half his lager and, taking the remote control off me, started flicking through the television channels.

'They could kill him. He-he's my nephew,' Mum pointed out.

Dad scratched his bristly chin thoughtfully. 'That's easy over there. I hear it's less than five hundred pounds nowadays. Stabbings used to be popular but now tablets are more fashionable.'

'Oh, that's all right then,' Mum said sarcastically. She gave him a look and then said cajolingly, 'I will go over there. I will speak to her.'

Mum got her way and another money order was sent to Auntie. That was months prior to sorting visas, legal papers and booking tickets to India.

Thankfully the great day of departure arrived. The usual amount of labelled luggage was loaded into the taxi's boot by the driver, while we stuffed ourselves inside it. For once, the train was packed. Standing close, Shyna and I sent coded texts to one another to make the journey pass fast.

After Mum's luggage covered the short distance between being tagged and put on the conveyor to disappear through the plastic flaps, we accompanied her to be frisked by security. As a female uniformed officer was patting down Mum's *salwar*-clad outside leg and up the inside, she beamed back at us, and said very loudly, 'My plan will get rid of them for good.'

Thankfully, she said it in Punjabi, otherwise there could have been a number of deductions that the airport authorities would have made; some good – some bad. And of course she may never have got to board her flight.

Startled, we looked at Dad. 'What plan? Dad, what's Mum talking about?' I asked.

'You'll find out when your mum gets back,' he replied and added, 'what are my lovely girls going to cook for their old Dad tonight? Only joking. How do you say, you know, when the cat is away...?'

Either side of him, we hooked an arm through his and urged him along. 'While the cat's away the mice will play,' Shyna said.

'A-ha. Tonight is special time off. So we get a takeaway,' he said. 'And we don't tell your mum.'

*

Our welcoming her back in Britain again was double-edged. We'd enjoyed Dad's *no rules,* but we'd missed Mum's strictness. Her cases by the wall looking like open-mouthed gargoyles; we sat together listening to Mum, and it was like the three weeks without her had never been.

'Jeevant's really in trouble. He's got in with the drugs cartel people from the next town. I had many long talks with the family. Everybody had ideas. Bring Jeevant here. Or to another of our family in America or Canada. Or marry him off so he becomes a man. Anyway, it's going to be difficult, but we can sort it all. Shyna, pass me my bag.' A quick rummage and Mum handed an envelope to Dad. His can of lager mid-way to his lips, never made it as she took it off him.

'What's this?' Perusing it, he burst out laughing. 'Hari Hound?'

'Are we getting a dog?' I asked excitedly. I had been expecting one every Christmas, just like in the adverts on television.

Dad pursed his lips as he scrutinised the paper without his glasses. 'Hm. *For all your life's complicated needs, there's Hari the hound here to help. Need help to find your other half? Missing information? No job too small or big. Just like bloodhounds, we sniff out the problem and get any job you need doing, done.*' He let out a laugh. 'There's lots of *needs* in that. What, because they *need* it d'you think?' He laughed again.

'Oh, does that mean we're not getting a dog then?' I asked, but was completely ignored.

Dad asked, 'And what's he going to do? You trust all this-this Hari stuff?'

'My gut said so. Dad went to Ludhiana with me specially to check them out and met Hari. He thought the trip worth doing.' Mum sounded self-satisfied.

It was Shyna that dropped the bombshell the next evening. Obeying parental orders I went to fetch her. Taking the stairs two at a time, my rushed entry to her room was foiled. The door was locked.

'Shyna, what you doing?' I pressed down on the handle and pushed but nothing budged. She never missed her favourite television soap. Hunkering down to peer through the keyhole, I just about made out her form on the bed. Not a good sign for someone as exuberant as her. Standing up and tapping lightly, I called, 'It's me.' All the locks in the house are well oiled so I barely heard it turn. She let me in then returned to her previous position. 'You okay?'

'I'm being married off.'

'You got to be kidding! You're not old enough. You're not are you? And they can't really make you...can they?' Her immediate thump on the pillow with balled fists spoke for her.

She snorted. 'Legal age is sixteen and I'm nearly that, and in two years you'll be too. And we'll find out then won't we!'

What a horrible thought. 'But...how do you know...I mean when did they tell you 'cause I've been around the whole time and...' I didn't want to believe it.

Undoing her plait, she scraped back her hair and started re-doing it tighter than necessary. 'They don't need to tell us do they...anyway, I heard Mum onto one of her friends and then she and Dad were arguing about it. That's her big plan, remember? You know what Mum's like, she'll make Dad do what she wants.'

'He doesn't always give in.' It sounded weak even to me. 'At least not every time.' With anything parent-related, Shyna and I were usually thinking on the same page. Mum could be evasive and talk with double-tongue, keeping everything open to conjecture. Dispiritedly slipping out of my pink rabbit-headed slippers, I joined her and sat lotus-style.

'She was saying, Mum that is, that she had heard good things about *the boy*. Makes sense now why Dad didn't go with her to India. He stayed behind to spy on us.' There was a catch in her voice. She rubbed at the point on her throat where it hurts if you stop yourself from crying. I always did the same.

'We'll have to get Dad on our side. Then they can't make us do anything we don't want to do.'

Shyna's look was disparaging. 'It's nothing to do with 'they'. You've been wanting a dog, and have you got one?

No, because Mum doesn't want all that mess and cleaning. She's the boss. I told you I thought they were up to something didn't I? And now the big day's here. That's probably why Auntie's visiting.' She twisted her lips exactly like Dad did, her voice bitter, 'For my wedding.' Pulling at my ponytail she thrust it away forcefully, stinging my skin. 'Get it?'

Nodding, I rubbed my cheek. 'And she's bringing – '

'Her son and a couple of his friends,' she interrupted. 'I haven't got much time. Wouldn't mind, but Dad doesn't even like any of them. It's all Mum's fault.'

I didn't understand what she was saying, but I felt the dread move along my legs. My feet had already gone numb. 'I don't think Dad will let it happen. Besides don't they come here after you've been over there to get married there? Not the other way around.'

'Doesn't matter. They'll make me. How can I embarrass them and say 'no'? I think the best thing is to pretend to be sick tonight. And in the morning they can't make me go to the airport with them. Then I'll pack and stuff.' All of a sudden energised, she sat up and said with alacrity. 'We know Mum puts her cash in the old toffee tin. You go get that while she's watching television and I'll check on-line.' She took a noisy breath. 'There's bound to be places for vulnerable girls. Plus we're Asian. Look, go back downstairs. Tell them I'm not feeling great. Tell them I...I've just been sick in the toilet. Just copy me in the morning okay?'

'I can't take Mum's money, and it's stealing.'

'If you don't we're going to starve. You want to die? We can't be sure we're going to find jobs straight away can we? Take just a bit then so she won't notice, eh? Look, I'm thinking on my feet here.'

I was about to tiptoe into Mum and Dad's room when Mum summoned us. Shyna motioned for me to go down while she hurried into the bathroom, locked the door and started coughing.

'Where's Shyna?' Mum asked.

'In the bathroom. I think she's not well. Feeling sick she said to say.' Whenever Mum looked at me I couldn't do untruths. Mum passed me on the stairs to check for herself.

I don't know how Shyna passed the lying-to-Mum test, but she was believed. It's a pity because as well as *Eastenders* she ended up missing out on her favourite dinner too. With the visitors from India coming, Mum had prepped loads. In addition to the *saag,* she'd made spicy lamb meatballs, and instead of *roti* to go with them, she did something unhealthy; *puris.* Dad and I made sure they didn't go to waste. I even beat him by eating three fresh green chillies to his one with my *dhal.* It was worth it because he gave me five pounds.

As the evening wore on, my stomach started churning and I just couldn't get myself to look at Mum and Dad. All I could think of was how much I'd miss them. When everything was cleared away and I told Shyna about Mum making a feast, she just laughed and said I wouldn't understand even if she told me, and then said, 'It's like the ritual of the last supper. I'm the sacrificial lamb.'

I had numerous suggestions ready to leap off my tongue, the prime-most one being telling Mum and Dad everything. In the morning, a very happy looking Mum forced a terrible looking Shyna to eat some dry toast. Acting like a martyr, Shyna nibbled and swallowed slowly, but did whisper, 'I'm starving,' as well as opportunistically grabbing quick bites of mine whenever Mum had her back to us.

'Girls hurry up! We're walking to the station, and what with them working on our line, we can't afford to miss our train,' said Dad. He was already wearing his coat.

'But Dad, I don't feel – ' said Shyna.

'Coat Shyna!' Mum interrupted with *the voice* and Shyna's was frozen. I followed suit hurriedly.

Safely ensconced and speeding towards Shyna's doom and gloom future, I couldn't help noticing the distorting effect of Mum's face reflected off the carriage window; with the slightest of movement her expression was Machiavellian, one minute angelic the next devilish. I nudged Shyna, drawing her attention to it. She nodded obliquely.

'You okay?' Mum asked Shyna. Caught off guard, my sister nodded. 'You tell me straight away if I have to get you anything. I'm going to need both of you well and helping me take care of our visitors.'

'Or we'll never hear the end of it.' Dad grinned, but Mum's glance wiped it off.

'Good.' Mum nodded, and the action caused her lime green and orange diamond patterned head scarf to slip. We had been waiting years to see it disappear, but its colours refuse to fade. Her brows knitted together in a frown. Tutting, she pulled it up, shooting a silencing glare at us as if knowing that one of us was going to comment on how the hideous thing matched nothing in her wardrobe. The remainder of the journey was made in silence by us, broken only occasionally by the comment from Dad about Hari Hound.

'Ten weeks is so long,' I couldn't stop myself from saying when we got to Heathrow airport. 'I mean...every day...' The enormity of what was about to happen had finally hit me.

'They are not going to be with us all the time. They'll be doing sightseeing. And going to stay with other relatives. Don't worry...it'll pass really quickly.' Dad's face didn't match his reassuring words or tone.

Shyna spoke up, 'Even with short stays with other relatives, it's still a lot of days spent at ours. Aren't they going to be stuck in their ways? Won't they turn us into their servants?'

My sister was right. Indian hospitality was hard work.

'You girls should have worn your Indian clothes.' Mum seemed distracted as she looked at the signs for directions. All of a sudden, she grabbed Dad's arm. 'We don't all need to go. It's only a few calls. I'll meet you back at that cafe,' she said, heading for the public telephones. She was gone for a long time, but when she joined us, she was like the feline who'd trapped her mouse and was anticipating the play to come.

'You managed to get through then?' Dad asked.

'Yes. Everything's sorted. I spoke to you-know-who.' She leaned forward and when we followed her cue, she laughed and touched my cheek. 'He said "be careful here and make sure we're not overheard. Just good precautions."'

'Okay...but are...ahem...arrangements in-hand here? Are they ready?' Dad whispered loudly.

'I went and checked. And Hari has been good. Efficient. All the information they need he's given them. Including what they'll find secreted. Just wait.' Mum looked over at the people queuing for food. 'I think I'm a bit hungry. Hm...a full English will keep me going until my sister and her entourage lands. Anyone else hungry? Shyna?'

We kept a close eye on the notice boards and were ready and waiting at the right place and time. Mum spotted her sister and managed a royal wave. The two young men nearest her were deep in conversation. They stopped briefly to cast an interested look in our direction.

I moved closer to Mum who put her arm around me. Something about them didn't feel right. I could feel the knot inside my stomach and the onslaught of indigestion. 'Mum, Shyna can't marry either of them,' I said urgently.

'Marry? Who said so? Of course she isn't.' Mum looked from me to Shyna. 'You're too young for a start. What on Earth makes...' She was looking in the distance. Airport security officers were leading the three newly arrived Asian people away.

'Right, time to go back and kill more time,' she said.

'What's going on Mum? Dad?' Shyna asked.

'The officers must suspect them of carrying something illegal and trying to sneak it into the country. Or, of course, something else they shouldn't,' Dad said. 'Not going too easy on whichever of them is the culprit, eh?' He winked at Mum.

'I totally agree with you.' Mum nodded. Hearing her mobile ring, she answered. 'Hello. Yes Hari. Oh yes. Exactly as you said. Into the luggage? Uh-huh. Very good. Thank you. There's no point in waiting for my sister is there?' She smiled back at Dad and pulled me close. 'Yes Hari. I'll definitely be recommending your unique services. The second half of the payment by bank transfer okay? Good. Bye bye.'

The End

THE FOUR P's:

THE PATHETIC POET, THE POORLY PATIENT, PROSTATE PETE AND THE PERSISTENT PISSER

ALEX WATSON

It's 02.44 am and the four-bed bay is silent. Alec has not had a wink of sleep. The guy in the bed opposite hurries out of bed every twenty minutes to go to the toilet. In apparent synchronised irritation, an unseen lady in another bay calls for a nurse halfway through the toilet cycle. Worst of all, his hydration has been delayed.

He presses the bell for help and is told no doctor has arrived. 'It's outrageous. Why am I in overnight if there are no bloody doctors in the hospital?'

He is still awake thirty minutes later. He sees a patient trundled in. Brian is covered in bandages and he is breathing through a tube. Alec tries to eavesdrop on the conversation but, apart from the word 'morphine', he can only pick up medical gobbledygook. Twenty minutes later he falls asleep.

It's still dark when a nurse prods him awake for his drip.

She hears an agonised groan from the next bay. Alec's drip will have to wait. He picks up snatches of muffled conversation. It doesn't sound good for the bandaged man.

The Persistent Pisser presses his buzzer and simultaneously hollers, 'Nurse! Nurse!'

He is ignored. Bandaged Brian has top priority. The Unrelenting Urinator presses his buzzer over and over. A second, yawning nurse ambles in. 'I've wet myself,' he whimpers.

Alec just stops himself yelling, 'You've managed to get to the loo half a dozen times already, so why not now?'

The nurse closes the curtains behind her and surveys the mess. She rolls her eyes upwards and starts peeling the bed.

By now Alex is wide awake. He watches as she emerges with a pile of sodden bed clothes. 'That's why you need a degree,' he chuckles and then hollers 'I need some sleeping pills.' There's no response. His simmering anger boils over. He recalls the words of his therapist. 'Write down situations that cause you anger and learn from them.' Alec struggled to complete the therapist's proforma because it meant articulating his feelings. He finds writing limericks gives him some release.

I have seen mich'lin man in his bed
With grey bandages over his head
His condition's forlorn
Will he last 'til the morn?
Seems a waste giving him all those meds

It is the afternoon and Alec complains to the patient on his right that he still awaits his operation.

'Stop winging, Alec,' pleads Prostate Pete. 'There's nowt to it. They shove some dye up your... up your arm and then they put you through the doughnut. That's what they call the scanner.'

Alec cringes. Thirty minutes later he goes to the loo only to find that The Woeful Wee Man is still in residence. He sneaks into the female loo.

The condition of Bandaged Brian has not improved. A few worried relatives visit. Nicey Nursey hurries over. He closes the curtains behind him. Alec gets out of bed and rummages around his locker. This is the ideal place to eavesdrop. He tunes in to the conversation greedily. He continues his locker exploration and is dismayed to find only a half sucked mint stuck to the bottom of the drawer. Clearly Brian is very ill indeed. Nicey Nursey leaves after providing what reassurance he can. The relatives remain round Brian's bedside trying to pick crumbs of comfort from Nursey's words. There is little to comfort them.

Alec soon loses interest and goes to the toilet taking his Daily Express, anxious to know which traitors are threatening a hard Brexit.

Ten minutes later a tall burly man emerges from the drawn curtains. The Terrifier finds Brian's bedside too claustrophobic and wants time to think. The Terrifier moves over to the window. The children's ward opposite blocks his view of the rolling hills beyond. He looks round in search of anything, absolutely anything, to distract him from Brian's condition. Maybe The Pathetic Patient will have a Playboy. The articles are always interesting. His eyes fall on the top of Alec's locker. He sees the open notebook and takes a quick look.

Alec returns from the toilet dragging his drip stand.

'You swine!'

'What?'

'Who do you think you are? How dare you say my brother's not worth treating? He's not dead yet, whereas you, my friend, better say your prayers.'

Alec backs off but there's nowhere to go. The Terrifier spots the drip stand with its five foot flex. That will do nicely, he thinks. He grabs the plug end of the flex and plans wrapping the rest around Alec's neck.

'Don't you dare come any closer,' pleads Alec. The Terrifier ignores him.

Prostate Pete shouts for help and tugs the alarm bell.

Nicey Nursey reaches the combatants and tries to slacken the flex which has already broken Alec's skin.

'Stay out of it. This is between me and him,' snarls The Terrifier, elbowing Nursey aside. Nicey Nursey utters an expletive which belies his name.

Alec and Nursey both struggle to overcome The Terrifier, but the bigger man remains in control. Alec loses strength and lets his grip slacken. He is gasping for his life.

Nursey desperately fights on. Three years at university didn't cover this situation. He eventually finds salvation in his father's Star Trek collection.

As Prostate Pete loves to relate afterwards, the No-Longer-Nicey-Nursey applies a Vulcan nerve pinch. Derek is immobilised. Nursey summons paramedics and then phones security.

A battered Alec is soon on his way to A&E.

*

With the protagonists gone, Prostate Pete strolls over to Alec's bed and starts to read the notebook.

Maybe Man Mountain went over the top but I see what got his goat, he ponders. Well two can play Alec's game. Prostate Pete has never attempted a limerick before but, after several crossings out, he is finally satisfied with his entry:-

So, that Alec is just not so smart
For his limerick cut back his bark
Now his windpipe's right sore
And he won't write no more
Except for Till Death Us Do Part.

The End

THE HAPPY WANDERER

ROSALIE ROSS

Yvonne experienced many different types of guest whilst working at the Inn. She vividly remembered one in particular who proved to be all calmness and self-control.

Morning coffee for the coach party was being served in the lounge when the faint clip-clopping of a horse's hooves could be heard approaching the Inn. A few minutes later, and smiling pleasantly, an elderly man entered reception and asked if there was somewhere suitable for his horse to be stabled overnight - and if so - was there a room available for him?

She thought that the dapper little man could have walked straight off the set of a Walt Disney film, blessed as he was with a fresh, glowing complexion, a pair of remarkably long ears, and clear, twinkling, deep set blue eyes that shone with health, vigour and intelligence. Glancing through the glass vestibule doors behind him, she was amazed to see a huge carthorse tethered to the rowan tree outside.

'Please take a seat,' she said, pointing at the nearby chair, 'I'll have to go and ask someone.'

She found Flora, the Housekeeper, sorting the laundry, and asked what should be done. The old lady often entertained her with amusing and sometimes alarming anecdotes about such wayfarers, describing them as, 'Adventurers; folk who like to travel on horseback. All through the hills they go, and are in no rush about it. They camp out when the weather's fine, but make for a friendly bed when they have need of a night's shelter and a good long soak. The horses stay in the outhouse; it's big and dry enough, and they can graze safely just by.'

The thought of these modern-day, cow-less cowboys had amused Yvonne. However, she held back from saying anything frivolous during one such conversation, having detected a note of admiration in her colleague's voice. Instead, doing her best to avoid using the term 'drop-outs' with its negative connotations, she ventured, 'They sound kind of hippyish - you know - free spirits.'

But Flora was quick in their defence. 'No lass. They're decent enough, harmless folk. No trouble, respectful and wise, clean and all; just stepping out of their lives for a while. You'll see all sorts, and the horses are no bother. But those nasty great motor bike contraptions...' She paused to shudder dramatically. 'Och, the noise! They're the ones that make the mess, grease marks all over the carpets, and if they don't take a bath, och, the smell of them ... dearie me! Just one night and the sheets are fuming. I was never so glad as when Mrs Mac changed to the laundry. When I think of all that soaking. Oh dearie, dearie me!'

On this occasion, she advised, 'Now, just you let him have the end single, and I'll get Hamish to bring some oats and hay when he picks me up. There's some in the outhouse already, but it won't harm to have fresh. We'll have to charge him mind; Mrs Mac puts another ten percent on the bill.'

This time, Yvonne was prepared, and despite Flora's reassurances and the man's wholesome appearance and polite manner, she made doubly sure to check the register against the dreaded *Black List* before offering him a room.

There was something particularly satisfying about leading him and his enormous companion around the back of the Inn. Soon, Flora appeared with a bag of apples and vegetables that she had managed to inveigle out of the kitchen, thanks to it being Niall's half-day.

And so it was, that, with the arrival of this strange, fairytale-like figure, Yvonne was to experience the first of many such modern-day rovers.

*

The following morning both rider and horse appeared to have been adequately refreshed and rested. Yvonne stood and watched the horse's plump flanks swaying almost hypnotically as the pair rode off at a leisurely pace, still holding in her hand the ten pound note the man had insisted upon paying for his room. She could only assume that he must have been a wealthy man indeed to be able to afford to give the equivalent of more than two and half weeks of her wages for just the one night's stay in a two star inn.

His room was clean and tidy when she went to strip and clean it soon after. He had even left half-a-crown tucked under the saucer of his early morning tea. She felt that he had more than made up for the financial and disturbing effects caused by the previous night's lost soul - who had soiled and ruined one of the new mattresses in a drunken stupor. The Inn might be over forty miles away from the nearest town, but somehow the world, with its problems and delights, had a way of reaching and affecting this remote and lovely place.

The End

NEW FAMILY

ROBYN CAIN

Dad has days when he goes off on one. 'Fashion thinks it controls market forces through the bull-shitting free press. They're not fooling us like they like to believe. Now of course, superstition is the new money. And look how no-hopers, like nature's runts, survive. Nature didn't intend that. Survival of the fittest...it's obvious.'

'I've got hopes,' I meow in protest.

'Think you'd better apologise to Lucky,' Mum says and strokes me.

'Sorry, Lucky. What I mean is, you should've been free. After all, you weren't planned so you're not a commodity. It's daylight robbery. Advertising costs millions and they blackmail us with sob stories. It's extortion.'

'Lucky. Shut your ears. Look dear, it was me with our Visa Card going for Lucky here,' says Mum. 'Nobody forced me to. It was my decision to go to a rescue centre.'

'But next door's cat had just had a litter. They were giving them away,' said Dad.

'We're all different. You avoid walking under ladders. Besides, I like black,' Mum says and strokes me again.

'You're both superstitious,' I meowed, adding that my precocious friend Mimi often waits for hours on the lookout to saunter across the paths of people just so she can get a reaction.

'You got time to steady the ladder so I can finish the window?' Dad asks.

Mum can multi-task and holds us both. I'm bored, so I make her sneeze by flicking my tail around her nose.

'Bless you!' shouts out Dad.

'It's my job to say that.' Annoyed, I hiss, bristle and claw Mum.

She says more than 'Ouch!' and loses her hold of the ladder in such a way that it slides. As a consequence Dad flies.

My name's Lucky and I am a bona fide member of this family. I know I have a majestic walk, so with head held high, I do so, satisfied that it didn't take me long to ensure that Dad was gone.

The End

ROMEO

HEBE GREEN

He hated his name with a vengeance. It was bad enough in primary school, now in high school it was torture. What were his stupid parents thinking of? Did they have some romantic notion that he would be famous one day? Who knows! They had separated when he was two, his Dad walking off to produce another child with another name totally unsuitable for its surroundings.

Romeo didn't have a lot of respect for anyone, let alone his family. To him they always seemed to be on the make, especially Uncle Jed who was in prison. The others were just a waste of space. But his mother was okay - even though she was a bit thick and could hardly read. He decided on action when he arrived home. His mother was out, yet again. Up in his small, cold room surrounded by the colour pink, (his mother had set her heart on a girl), he covered himself with blankets. He began to write. If he had one talent in life, it was writing.

He would go and take something for himself; after all, he had nothing to lose. He knew where all his fellow pupils lived. He listened carefully when they talked about their homes and when they went out. He began to make a list. James was going to be the first; snotty James, who thought he was better than anyone else, just because he lived in a detached council house. He had a big dog, but apparently it wouldn't harm a fly. Great! Tonight was the night. The minutes ticked by.

His mother arrived home and called up at him. As usual, she had stopped off at the local chippie, 'Romeo! Come and get your tea.'

He just needed to add a few more names to the list: Badger…Craig…Stuffy…

'ROMEO!'

'Okay! Coming.'

*

He had a horrendous time at school the next day, which made him even more determined to put his plan into action. He would show them that they weren't the only ones with laptops and tablets; he wasn't going to tell them that his mother never had enough money for those kinds of 'useless objects', as she always shouted. 'Cigs were a bad price these days without forking out for rubbish like that.'

She was engrossed in *Coronation Street.* He stood and stared at her for a moment, thinking how easily led and unlucky she was as he left the house later that evening. It was damp outside and he pulled his scarf tight around his mouth. A man was pulling his dog roughly along and he immediately felt sorry for the poor creature.

'Come on Stanley!' the man bellowed. *Sad Stanley* was dragged away from his tree before he had finished relieving himself. Romeo knew he had to get away before he kicked the man. His mission was serious. Get on with it, he chided himself.

*

For the next three nights Romeo was in his element. He would don his hood and thick clothes and sneak out to *visit* the boys' houses. There was a lot of talk at school about where those who still had electrical goods were hiding them. He was surprised how easy it was; especially when he came across some loud TV's and unlocked back doors. So far, he had collected three tablets and one laptop.

Another two nights and he would have all he wanted. It couldn't be simpler; he was a born robber! This stealing could be done quickly and his mother hadn't noticed his absences. He never felt guilty, nor used the goods he stole. What was going on with him he didn't know, just that he gained a lot of satisfaction from it all.

*

The weather had turned nasty and everything was to change that snowy evening. Everyone was rushing inside after covering their cars with old towels and blankets. But he still went out. Then he saw *Sad Stanley* being pulled about again and made a mental note to steal him later on. He turned when he heard the dog whimper and saw the man kicking the poor creature. Unable to stop himself, he blurted out, 'Oi! Stop that!'

The man gave him a hostile look and shouted back, 'Mind your own bloody business!'

Romeo felt himself becoming brave. 'Why are you so nasty to him? You never give him time to finish. You're cruel. That's what you are, a nasty, cruel man…'

Shocked, the man stood and stared at the youth. Then his temper got the better of him as he threw Stanley's lead down and began to walk away. 'Oh yeah! You have the damn dog then. There! He's all yours and you're welcome to him.'

Romeo stood and watched the man's back disappear around the corner, then slowly approached the shivering dog and picked up the lead. Somehow he knew, even then, that he would never, ever, abandon him. It didn't matter what fuss Mum made.

But now, he was on a mission. Everything around him was covered in a thick layer of snow and looked somehow unfamiliar as he coaxed Stanley to walk beside him.

For a while, he became disorientated and managed to lose his bearings, making him wonder if he was outside the rear of the house that was his target for that night. The back gate was wide open, so was the back door, which surprised him.

He patted Stanley and told him to be quiet and wait as he tied his lead to the nearby drainpipe. As usual, the TV was on. This was brilliant! It was all ready for him to go in and take his pick. Flakes of snow circled and fell inside the kitchen, and then, he didn't know why, he began to feel a little uneasy. Some food was burning on the stove and he slipped in and turned the gas off. But then his flight mechanism jumped into action when he heard someone, or something, making a whimpering noise nearby. Managing to control himself, he crept into what turned-out to be the living room; a cold, dark place, lit only by a small TV. His blood ran cold when he saw that the whimpers were coming from an elderly woman who was tied to a chair, her hands and feet tightly bound. Without thinking, he rushed in and began to untie her.

'Thank you. Thank you,' she sobbed repeatedly, clinging onto him afterwards.

He covered her with an old quilt off the settee and managed to calm her down. Then, still shaking himself, he made her a cup of tea before ringing for the police.

*

'He must have got cocky and decided to go for money instead,' the constable said, sometime later. 'You've done your bit and can go now, son. Looks like the old girl just needs checking over. The ambulance will be here soon enough.'

However, Sarah, 'the old girl' had regained her composure, and spoke-up softly but firmly. 'Not on your Nelly! I want the lad to stay with me. You can cancel it; I'm not going to any hospital.'

*

Sarah had two spare bedrooms. She had been very lonely. and so life looked up for Romeo and his mum - forever and ever. They made a great family. His mum blossomed under Sarah's guidance and even had a bit of money to spare, enough to keep *Glad Stanley*, the new name he was given, in warm and patient comfort.

The Tablet Thief was never found, and all the stolen items mysteriously reappeared in their own places.

And that is how Romeo learned to like his name – now that he had become a hero!

The End

'LET THERE BE LIGHT'

A TRUE STORY

ROSALIE ROSS

And God said, 'Let there be light,'
and there was light.
God saw that the light was good,
and he separated the light
from the darkness.
(Genesis 1:3,4).

By the time I was 28 I had glanced at these words, as I had a good proportion of the Old Testament, and decided that, like the rest of the archaic book, they had nothing to do with life on Earth now, and certainly nothing to do with me. How wrong could I have been.

They tell me that I was a happy and outgoing child - that was until I had my first conscious meeting with my father, which happened when I was four. One day, a man dressed in a soldier's uniform and carrying a heavy kitbag, walked into my grandparent's house where I had always lived with my mother, brother and sister. Naturally surprised, I asked, 'Who are you?'

'Your father,' he replied, dropping the kitbag and moving towards me. He then began to hit me - hard, only stopping when I vomited.

Soon after, we left the quiet Welsh town I had always known, and moved hundreds of miles away to live in the unfamiliar and strange environment of a noisy Army camp.

(I should explain that my parent's marriage had been going through an extremely difficult phase for several years, not helped by the effect of my father's war experiences and his continued lengthy and unaccompanied overseas postings.)

And so it seemed to me that all the light quickly faded from my world as I struggled to understand what was happening to and around me. We three children quickly became fearful, and then terrified of this stranger who had come to live amongst us, and who was now verbally and physically attacking us on a regular basis. It didn't matter if he was stone cold sober or blind drunk; our cries only seemed to increase his anger, as did all forms of emotionalism. And so we also learned how to keep quiet - and swallow hard.

One of his favourite forms of *amusement* was to hold one of my knees in a vice-like grip whilst manipulating the kneecap out of position. He subjected my mother and myself to this form of torture. We would be frozen to the spot, unable to move; the pain was all encompassing. Not surprisingly, we soon began to experience chronic pain, which was put down to arthritis in my mother's case, and growing pains in mine.

*

A particularly upsetting event occurred when I was ten. By now, my younger sister had been born, my father had been demobbed, and we were living in rural East Anglia. I was attempting to run in a school race when my left leg felt as though it had exploded beneath me. The local doctor diagnosed ligament or tendon trouble. A crepe bandage was applied, aspirin given, and a few week's rest ordered. It took a long time to get back on my feet and teach myself to walk again. Years later, I learned that my kneecap had fractured.

You may be asking: 'Where was my mother all this time?' Well, she was trying to survive herself whilst bringing up four children, now seriously weakened by regular beatings, chronic asthma, frequent bouts of bronchitis, and living in constant fear. I don't know if she was aware of the work of the NSPCC, and back in the 1950's there was no ChildLine or women's refuges. All she could think of doing was to ask the Army Chaplain for help. His response was to tell her to pray. He also told her that, if she did leave her husband, her children would be taken away from her. This was no exaggeration, because when she became seriously ill and was taken to hospital soon after, we were removed and placed in an Army orphanage. For several months we were allowed to believe that she had died and, desperately unhappy, tried our best to cope in the harsh, disciplined environment. When she learned where we were, and ill though she still was, she discharged herself and came to the orphanage and demanded our release. Unfortunately, our relief and joy at the reunion was short lived when we found ourselves back home - and with our father again.

*

Time passed. Desperate to escape my home environment, at the age of 17, I applied for, and was accepted, by the Women's Royal Air Force. The retired doctor who performed my entrance medical declared that, 'I had a bit of housemaid's knee,' and that 'a bit of square-bashing would do me good.' A few weeks into Basic Training, and whilst marching with my flight on the parade ground, the once fractured kneecap shattered and splintered into several pieces. The Air Force surgeons were wonderful at patching me up, so much so that I was able to start training as a nurse a year later. However, the other knee began to cause problems, and I was eventually given a medical discharge at the age of 21, with, for the medically inclined, a diagnosis of:- *'Left patellectomy. Severe, bilateral chondromalacia patellae.'*

Unwilling to return home, and needing a job with accommodation, I began working in hotels and holiday camps in various roles: chalet maid, barmaid, children's nanny, and booking clerk/receptionist. I sought affection from wherever I could get it, even though every relationship would eventually turn sour. Looking back, I realise that I was attracted to – and attracting – men who were as damaged as I was, if not more so.

Every so often I would try to get back into nursing, and succeeded on two separate occasions. However, I had to give up on that dream when I began developing blood clots in both knees and the remaining kneecap finally shattered. More surgery followed, after which I was informed that the hospital could not employ me anymore. Just before I left, Mary, one of the other nurses, gave me a small, black leather-bound Bible. I had been impressed by her, especially by the way she seemed able to handle life's ups and downs with such serenity. We all knew she was *religious,* and out of curiosity, I went with her to church once, but the experience seemed to go over my head; the whole religion thing was a complete mystery to me.

*

By the time I was 24 my spine had started to give me a lot of problems. I knew I was on the road to nowhere; even so, I managed to gain a place on a one year shorthand typing course. Afterwards, and still a victim to my constant restlessness, I returned to hotel work, preferring anywhere in the Scottish Highlands. However, as my condition deteriorated, I was forced to accept the fact that I needed to find a less physically demanding way of life. And so, with a sinking heart, I returned home and back to office work.

At the age of 28 I was in constant pain and fearful of even more painful surgery. It seemed that no matter how hard I tried to sort myself out, it was just not meant to be. The fates were not on my side; I believed myself to be jinxed. Exhausted by the struggle, I felt that there was no point in going on and calmly took the decision that if nothing good happened for me soon, I would put an end to it all.

Every so often, and especially during times of extreme boredom and incapacity, I would read a page or two of the little black book Mary had given me. I had come to look upon it as a good luck charm, ineffectual though it seemed to be. By now, I had reached *The Book of Job,* and the poor man's suffering struck a chord with me.

One day, after reading a short passage, something strange happened. An image of Mary's face came clearly into my mind. I remembered how she had tried to tell me something about God. Well, it was worth a try! I looked up and focused on a corner of the ceiling, feeling that, if He did exist, He must be up there somewhere. I was angry and desperate, and recall saying that He had better do something - quickly. I would give Him a week. I had a strong sensation that I had been heard.

My curiosity mounting, I even found out where a local pastor lived and knocked on his door one evening to ask if he could explain something about God to me. Obviously surprised, he invited me in and read a few verses about choosing light over darkness out of his Bible. I didn't understand and came away even more bewildered. By now, I really wanted to find out more about this God, and recall kneeling, painfully, beside my bed one evening and pleading that He make Himself known to me.

I was able to return to work the next day. Then I remembered that a group of *religious* people held a weekly lunchtime prayer meeting in one of the company's empty offices. Feeling slightly embarrassed, I went to sit at the back for the last ten minutes of their next session. One of them approached me afterwards and offered a couple of free tickets to a Christian event for the following weekend.

And so, that was how I came to be sitting amongst a large crowd in a huge marquee on the grounds of a Methodist Bible College, deep in the heart of the Derbyshire countryside a few days later. A young evangelist was speaking, and somehow it felt as though he was talking to me personally.

He told us how God requires justice, and that someone had to pay the price for all our sins. I didn't need telling that I was a sinner; all the years of pain and guilt were weighing down heavily on me. He explained how Jesus had allowed Himself to be crucified in our place.

This was the first time I heard the Gospel: that God's very own Son had come to Earth to show us His Father's love and restore our broken relationship with Him; in so doing, He had taken *my* sins upon Himself and taken *my* place on the Cross. Now the way was clear for me to know God. I was equally disturbed and astonished at this news. But God must have given me the gift of faith then: the faith to believe that what I had just heard was true. And I knew that I had to do something about it.

For most of my life I had reigned-in all my emotions, and I was determined not to let them loose now, especially in such a public setting. However, when the evangelist held one arm out, and said, 'I would like to introduce you to Someone; Someone Who died to meet you,' all I can say is that I was very aware that Jesus was standing right there next to him - and looking at *me!* He was holding His arms out. 'Come. Come to me now,' He said. I could see tears in His eyes. Shocked, and not knowing what to do, I sat and stared at, what I can only describe, as a deeply moving and private vision.

I had no notion what an altar call was, and when the evangelist invited all those who wanted to ask Jesus into their hearts to leave their seats and go to the front, I held back when others went forward. I couldn't do *that!* Then they began to sing *Just As I Am.* I had never heard the hymn before, but God used the words to break down my pride, fear and stubbornness when, by the fourth verse, a sense of peace came over me, and I left my seat and calmly went to join the others at the front. We knelt as the evangelist prayed for us. And now I cried – and I wasn't afraid to.

Afterwards, we were taken into the nearby chapel where it was carefully explained to us what had just happened. Then I prayed *The Sinner's Prayer,* slowly and thoughtfully. My counsellor told me that because I had sincerely repented and really wanted Jesus in my life, God had forgiven and accepted me. He was my *Heavenly* Father now and I was part of a new family: His Church. In effect, I had been *born again.* And that was how it actually felt, because I knew, absolutely *knew* that I had been found. I had been rescued. That was when I became aware that Light had broken into my dark existence, and that Light was none other than Jesus Himself.

The Lord guided me to a Bible-Believing church the very next Sunday and I began to know what it was to be His child. Life was still far from easy; the Devil threw some very nasty things my way. But now I was walking with Jesus and had Christian brothers and sisters loving and supporting me. It was a strange – but wonderful – thing, this new life, especially when I began to experience effective and permanent emotional and physical healing.

*

After a few years I felt that I needed to contact Mary. I wanted to thank her and let her know how The Lord had used her faithfulness in trying to tell me about Him and in giving me that Bible. I had no idea where she was, so I wrote a letter and sent it to the hospital where we had both nursed. Some kind person read it and forwarded it on to her, and I was thrilled to receive a reply from her some time later. She told me that she was married and working as a missionary in Nigeria, and that my letter just happened to arrive at a time when she was in need of some encouragement in her ministry.

I, too, had married, having met my husband five years after becoming a Christian. His first wife had died recently, leaving him alone to bring up their two young sons, aged three and four. Through all the pain, this once hardened atheist had had his own dramatic encounter with Jesus.

My first sight of him was when he was standing at the edge of a pool before stepping in to be baptised. Looking at him, I had an almost overwhelming sensation of The Lord saying to me, 'Look at your husband,' which was a shock, because by now I was a confirmed spinster! But the Lord knew best, and just one year later I was given a package deal when we were married – and I became a very naïve new wife and stepmother.

And what about my other father, my human one? Well, that's another story; but I can tell you that Jesus helped me to understand, and eventually, to forgive him. By freeing him, I discovered even more freedom myself.

*

I have been in the care of my Heavenly Father for the best part of forty years now; walking – yes, still walking – with Him, in His Way and in His Light. This Father has never hurt or rejected me. He has limitless understanding, compassion and patience. His love is constant. He freely pours His grace, love and strength into me. There have been plenty of hard times along the way, but that's life! But I can honestly testify that Jesus picks me up and carries me at such times; there is absolutely no doubt about it.

I'm sure you will understand why I love this Scripture, and make no apologies for repeating it here:-

And God said, 'Let there be light ' and there was light.
God saw that the light was good,
and he separated the light from the darkness.
(Genesis 1:3,4).

And He did!
And He does.
What a Father.

The End

MONSIEUR HENRY
(THROUGH THE EYES OF A CHILD)

ALEX WATSON

Janey waited until she heard the ping of the microwave downstairs. Dad was heating one of his disgusting ready meals. She had the night to herself.

She opened the zipped pocket of her rucksack and took out the letter that had been shouting to her since lunchtime. She examined the address forensically, squeezed her eyes and, after one failure, was able to memorise it. She might have to ditch the letter quickly. That partly depended on what was inside. Janey prayed this wouldn't be necessary. She envisaged dangling this precious keepsake in front of the other gang members each time they met.

Je t'aime had formed only one month before and had but one aim – to collect as much material as possible on M. Henry, their French teacher. The catalyst for the gang was one of M. Henry's lessons. He was teaching the word order of the French for *I love her*.

He explained that the abbreviated pronoun came before the verb rendering '*Je l'aime.*'

One of the regular wags stage-whispered, 'The Hunchback of Notre Dame.'

The other boys roared with laughter at the apparent answer '*Je lame.*' Unaware of the multilingual pun, M. Henry stumbled on.

The girls glared at the boys' immaturity then turned to their heartthrob. They all swore afterwards that he was looking directly at them when he added *'Je t'aime.'* There was a collective gasp for air. Then, for the benefit of the slower learners (the boys), he breathed 'I love you.'

No Baptist teacher from the Deep South could have converted so many in that instant. Imbued with a common fervour, the girls echoed his words in unison with unconfined passion. This was a day they would never forget. This was one French sentence they would never forget. The bell saved M. Henry's blushes and he departed *tout de suite.*

A month on, M. Henry had let slip a *double entendre* which caused the whole class to gasp in mock horror. Once again the bell came to his aid. In his haste he dropped an envelope he had been reading during a verb exercise. Janey, who had won the battle to sit in front of their adored teacher, snatched the envelope before anyone else could notice.

*

Janey took a deep breath and prised the letter from the envelope. The contents were better, much better, than she had dared hope. Barclays Bank was asking M. Henry to confirm his personal details before processing a loan application. To Janey, the words *personal details* had an intimacy the bank had never intended. She read:

Full name: M. Albert Jacques Henry. Albert, she thought, so Victorian. Albert, on the other hand, pronounced *en français,* sounded sexier.

Address : 40 Elgin Court. The posh estate? He must be loaded. Some people have it all. *Telephone (home)* 0141 496 5806. OMG! His phone number. No way am I going to share that with anyone she thought.

Without a care, Janey picked up her mobile but stopped dialling after the area code.

What will I say? she lamented, this needs some thinking about. Janey was in a quandary. She desperately wanted to boast about her discovery to the rest of the gang.

Her knowing that M. Henry was Albert, and knowing where he lived would put Olivia, the gang leader's nose, out of joint and could even knock her off her perch. Tomorrow night, she decided, I'll phone then.

*

Janey waited impatiently for her mother, Rachael, to make her nightly phone call home.

Come on, Mum, get a move on! Why did you take a job that involved working away from home? It's so selfish, she spat.

At last, the call came.

'Hi Janey, love.'

'Hi.'

'What sort of day have you had, darling?'

'Fine.'

'Oh, before I forget, did you remember to pay for your day trip? Dad did give you the money, didn't he?'

'Uh-huh.'

Rachael was becoming suspicious of her daughter's terse responses. It was time for an open question. 'What did the geography teacher say about calculating the diameter of the Earth?'

'Too busy.'

'Janey, what's wrong darling? You're generally such a chatterbox.'

'I'm fine Mum. I've got a ton of homework to do. Got to go.' Thank God that's over, mused Janey. Now for my chat with Albert.

She unpinned her *One Direction* poster to reveal her prized collection of *Instagram* photos of M. Henry. Her gaze settled, as it always did, on the photo of her hero coming down the main steps, smiling directly at her. She took her phone from her pocket and paused. One more run-through, she thought. Looking directly at her smiling Albert and with only her first teddy, Hairy Beary, as an audience, she ran through her script.

'Bon jour, Monsieur Henry.' Scolding herself for messing up so early, she started again. *'Bon soir, Monsieur Henry.'*

'Bon soir, mademesoille. Who I am speaking to?'

'It's Janey, *Monsieur Henry,* class 7B.'

'Oui, oui, *la belle* Janey. How can I help you?'

'Sorry to bother you but I'm stuck with my homework. I can't get my head around when to use *tu* and when to use *vous.'*

There were some blank lines in the script here. Janey couldn't anticipate exactly what M. Henry would say. In any case, she wasn't entirely sure of the correct answer only that how great it would be if the short telephone conversation ended with...

'If expressing my feelings for you, Janey, I would say, *Je t'aime.'*

'Je t'aime, aussie, Albert.'

'A bientôt.'

Hairy Beary regarded her with disdain but Janey was satisfied. She punched speed dial #1. *'Bon soir, Monsieur Henry.'*

A woman's voice hollered, ''Oi, Albert, some Frenchie's on the blower.'

Janey's heart felt like it wanted to jump into her mouth. Shocked, she banged the phone down and squeezed Hairy Beary as tightly as she could.

The End

DUTY FREE

ROBYN CAIN

The news blaring from the radio moved from telling listeners about cricket and India's chances against Britain, to the most interesting court case they'd had in the last decade. It was the first time the broadcast had come across the airwaves clear and crackle-free. With a couple of swift strides Ram Singh had reached it and switched it off.

'I wanted to hear that,' Ram's father said. A little frown marred the handsome features.

'They're only repeating what they said an hour ago, dear,' his wife mentioned and smiled across the room at Ram.

'It upset you last time. But if you want I'll switch it back on?' Ram offered.

'Never mind,' Mr Singh said without looking up from his reading.

At just over twenty-one, Ram desperately wanted to follow in his father's footsteps. Except that they were huge and he took after his mother in stature. However, neither of his parents had allowed him to be deterred. They were amazing parents and had worked hard for him. And today he was experiencing a pre-state of being. To please them, he'd worked hard. He wanted to give them a better life. One where they wouldn't have to continue toiling until there was no more time left to rest and enjoy what they'd striven for. He never wanted to hear them emit sighs of regret. Ram hoped he hadn't got it wrong because now, finally, the culmination of all that effort was about to happen. He had been, seen and hunted for. And in three days time, with all the evidence played out in front of them, the jury would be out and a final decision on his life – and without a doubt theirs too – made.

The car waiting with its engine turning was a black, four door saloon. A vehicle that was in a different league to his past modes of travel that included the local buses, rickety rickshaws, taxis and his faithful bicycle. Two severe-faced uniformed officers waited to escort him. It had been decided that these trials were of such importance that chances couldn't be taken and the mobs mustn't be allowed to catch his scent at any cost. It was time to go. 'Mum, Dad, this is it.' Hovering by the door he added, 'Don't forget...you'll be there won't you?'

'We won't forget, son. Your father and I will both be there to support you. And I'll try not to cry. But I cannot promise.' His mother knew how significant it all was. In fact, it was a sort of threshold where dreams were made or broken. Where prayers asking for deliverance might be answered, but it didn't depend on whose were the most fervent, the most fervently delivered, nor the bargains offered in exchange for their fulfilment.

He exchanged a final look with his mother. It was message-laden, expressing depths of feeling that could never be voiced by a boy recently-become-a-man in anyone's presence. His reputation had to be upheld. His father was the one person whom he didn't mind referring to their mother-son bond, because the same also existed between the two men.

'Look at them in their special world,' Ram enunciated loudly enough so that even his father, whose hearing was in a rapid decline, was able to hear him.

He'd caught his mother, who hated seeing time wasted, nervously stuffing a large canvas bag with all possible items related to her embroidery that she might need during the long hours of sitting and watching patiently. Realising she'd been discovered, she'd smiled nervously and said, 'Just in case the day over-runs.'

'Mum, you're not going to be able to concentrate if you do that stuff. And you know people will be watching you also. Sometimes even more than they are me.' He immediately regretted saying that because she then frenziedly started preparing the cauliflower and potato curry to cook for them after they returned. While the diced onions, garlic and ginger sizzled, she chopped the remaining ingredients. 'Mum, for goodness sake, leave it. You work too hard!'

'Son...' A word and a look said it all. Only once the pan's lid was firmly in place was she satisfied. When they first got married her husband told her his food had to be freshly cooked every day. She'd managed it thus far. No matter how their lives changed, there had to be some stability. And if this was their one constant, then it wasn't a bad thing to have she often reminded Ram.

There was a firm knocking on their door. 'Ram...go! And be quick-witted.'

She waved at her son. It wouldn't have ranked highly amongst others, but he'd been seeing that since he was a child. For him it evidenced that she knew he was afraid and he must be strong. Ram pocketed her response in a compartment in his mind. 'You will make sure Dad comes too? Even if he doesn't want to and says...well, you know.' At her nod, he closed the door on them. Three pairs of soles crunched down the path and away from the house where he'd been born.

Mrs Singh spoke to her husband without turning to look at him, because her gaze was fixed upon the window that looked out onto the world outside. A part of her wanted her son to return into the sanctuary of the family home where he'd never have to suffer extremes of indignity or jubilation. The other portion knew it was best the cord had finally been cut. 'Would you like to go and get dressed dear? You know how long it takes you to prepare. I already set your suit out for you, and your favourite shirt is pressed.' When Mr Singh didn't answer, she touched his arm, repeated a segment of her statement, 'Go and get dressed dear,' and then picked up the photograph of their family, wiping it free of dust with the corner of her *chooni.*

'Not yet,' he replied.

'My dearest, do you remember how long it took for our families to permit us to be alone together?' Mrs Singh sighed. 'So very long! And that was only after they saw how well trained I was in housework. So many years ago it seems now.'

'Oh, not so many at all,' Mr Singh said, looking up briefly from the tome he was reading. 'This is a very excellent book.'

'You said so yesterday. And for the past month, since it was your birthday in fact.'

He held it up and looked at the cover suspiciously. 'Really? But I only started it this morning.'

Mrs Singh eased the book out of his grasp. 'It is indeed a very good book. You can read some more later. You need to wash and shave. We can't let our son down by being late.'

Mr Singh looked up at her and smiled. 'You're always looking at that photo. Is it because you like looking at me or that you like looking at the Prime Minister? You know that my mother said you were only marrying me because of my cricketing prospects.'

'Well I didn't because prospects are as elusive as dreams. Please go get dressed.'

'Very well. But I hope you don't intend to take me to see the team play. If I haven't been picked to play this season, and I don't think I have otherwise they'd have been in touch by now, then I have no intention of going to see the look of satisfaction only rivals' faces. You will always be proud of me though won't you?'

'Nothing will ever stop me being proud of you,' Mrs Singh told him and gently pushed him towards the doorway.

'Who was that young man that left? He's not one of Ram's new teachers is he? They get younger and younger it seems.'

Swallowing the lump in her throat, Mrs Singh injected a little lightness into her voice and said, 'He came to give us an invite to go watch *him* play cricket. And your rivals aren't going to be there. So just go and get yourself ready to take me out. It's one of the promises you made upon proposing to me.'

'I did, didn't I? How can you even doubt that I'd forget!' He kissed her cheek and left.

She looked at the clock. Soon a taxi would be arriving to take them to watch their son who was freely, dutifully, following in his father's footsteps. When the team's manager had told her that it wouldn't be long before Ram would be scoring victorious runs for their country, he had said nothing at her bitter sweet smile. She knew he understood that life gave and it took.

'Making a space on the mantelpiece for another photograph isn't going to be difficult,' she'd replied.

The End

MEGA-BITTEN

RUBY WELLINGTON

According to my calendar, (a paper one that hangs on my wall) my uncle's birthday is approaching, so I make my way to a phone shop for a present.

I very rarely venture into town, only when necessity demands do I make the journey and nearly always return despondent and often confused, like an alien who has crash landed on an unknown plant. However, confident that I knew what type of phone was required, I thought the transaction would be reasonably smooth. My only reservation was whether they would stock a basic model.

The first thing I explain to the youthful salesperson is that I want to view phones that are only capable of sending text messages and making phone calls, and use words like *basic* and *simple*. I am shown a whole wall of phones. I then explain that I require a phone that cannot, with the best will and determination in the world, connect to any internet. I see the penny drop as the assistant moves me to two phones. Another assistant comes to join us; this was what I was afraid of: a two pronged attack. They have realised that their commission on this sale would be minimal, and this saps the enthusiasm out of them. I understand that I am the curiosity, and that they don't meet many customers like me.

On viewing the phones, I pick one; satisfied that the phone is as basic as possible. I notify the pair.

One of them confirms, 'This is for a pay as you go, no contract deal.'

At this point, one of the assistants goes to the stock room out the back. The remaining assistant engages me in a monologue of sales spiel from their training day. Seeing me glaze over, he moves away.

Then I hear a voice, 'Are you with us?'

'Excuse me?' I reply, thinking, did I just faint or do something to warrant this question.

She replies, 'Are you with us already?'

I am confused as she is standing at the desk and I am a little distance away, sitting down. I would have expected her to move closer to me rather than call across the shop.

I replied, 'I don't even know who you are.'

I hear a mental tut, but she manages to suppress laughter until the other assistant joins her, and then I hear whispers. Unable to look me in the eye, I am summoned to the desk while they complete the paperwork; although I see no paper in sight, only a computer screen.

From the corner of my eye I see an elderly woman sitting down with another assistant. The youth is in full flow; 'Upgrade ..blah texts, megabytes, contract, blah lala blah, apps, pixels, …'

We share a glance that says; 'I cannot understand a single word that is being spoken to me.' I have landed on planet Pluto.

A head appears from round the screen and I am asked for my phone number and address. I feel I need to explain again that I am not signing up for a contract, only a phone. She nods to impress on me that she is aware of this, but remains poised over the screen for my information.

'Do you really need to have my details? I would much rather not give them,' I reply.

'No-one ever looks at them, we just need them to register the phone,' the assistant responds.

Well, I'm thinking, 'if no-one looks at them, then why the need for me to give you them?

Now the supervisor, (I assume as she has an air of authority) senses my reluctance, and explains, 'We have to complete this information so the company is satisfied that it is a genuine sale, and not a made up one.'

What a strange idea that someone would make up a sale. Still, I need further assurances. 'You're not going to use my phone number -'

'No, it's just for the record.'

'Or pass my details on to any other company -'

'No.' The supervisor almost sighs, and this does not give me confidence that she understands my need for anonymity.

I am handed my bag of merchandise, which I receive with a *thank you.* These last twenty minutes have been confirmation that marketing is no longer about the customer's needs, rather about sales spiel. I am resigned to the fact that not only has the world of technology left me behind, but communication appears to have become problematic too.

I wonder, are we living in times where the capitalist system is like a large baby that needs constant feeding while it produces a multiple of hungers; like the ancient pagan gods who were appeased by sacrificing babies? This system also creates casualties. I feel like a casualty, until I see a homeless man sitting in an empty shop doorway. This is more subtle than a sacrificed baby, but nonetheless still unacceptable. No doubt he started life with hopes and has ended up being judged as *economically unviable.*

However, the homeless man told me that he owns four properties and has a title of *Earl,* and yet I see an absence of socks and shoe laces.

Well, Christmas is fast approaching … that will keep the system churning.

The End

WHEN MY BELL TOLLED

ON THE 13TH ANNIVERSARY
OF MY HEART TRANSPLANT

ALEX WATSON

The Gift of Life – there is none higher
The donor's kin, I must admire
For their dear son has joined his Maker
Yet he lives on as heart of stranger.

The Gift of Life – this rhyme I utter
To celebrate a wife none better
My pride in wedding of my daughter
Delight in son's, across the water.

The Gift of Life – near death I sought her
I now rejoice in two granddaughters
When my bell tolled, I heard a stranger
Who pulled me from the final danger.

The Gift of Life – the highest honour
A gift sublime from one young biker
I thank each day where'er I wander
And try my best to do him honour.

*

ABOUT THE AUTHORS

ALEX WATSON

Alex loved his family and his native Scotland, especially the sound and swirl of the bagpipes. A talented writer, he became the editor of the student magazine whilst at the same university where he met his wife. Later, when the children came along, his creative side was expressed in writing a series of stories for their bedtime reading.

There followed a long and varied career at Barclay's Bank, which was unexpectedly cut short. He underwent and survived a heart transplant at Wythenshawe Hospital, after which, and extremely grateful, he characteristically became a volunteer, eventually taking on the role of Public Governor with responsibility for England (apart from the Greater Manchester Area).

For the next fifteen years Alex tried to live life to the full. Amongst his various ventures, he joined several creative writing groups. BEYOND THE BRACKETS was one such group, and is proud to testify how much its members appreciated, benefitted from, and enjoyed his hallmark razor sharp wit.

HEBE GREEN

Hebe has always led a challenging and busy family life and is still heavily involved in caring for some of her four grandchildren. She is a keen life-long learner, confirmed by studying for and achieving a BA in Humanities in her forties whilst helping her family renovate a farmhouse in Normandy.

Travelling has always been an important part of her life; she has visited many parts of Europe and even toured New Zealand in a campervan.

She is a committed member of several groups, one of which involves using the internet to teach basic English to children in India. She also finds time to paint, walk, keep fit and sing in a local choir. Another important aspect of her life is creative writing, which is something she finds pleasurable and as a useful means of self-expression.

EVE GREY

Eve Grey was born in France and moved to England when she was four years old. Now aged fifteen, she lives in Cheshire with her family.

She loves horse riding, music, going to combat classes and gym training.

A prolific story teller from a very early age, her first book was self-published when she was still at primary school. Since then, she has contributed to various anthologies. Like all serious writers, she has an interesting relationship with her fictional characters.

RUBY WELLINGTON

Ruby Wellington was born in Brisbane, Australia, where she spent her first few years travelling with her missionary parents. The family needed to return to the United Kingdom and her father found employment as an underground train driver. She enjoyed London, but now lives in Cheshire.

Living in a Victorian house, Ruby loves old and second hand items, especially clothes. Even her rescue animals and foster children have all been pre-loved.

Having gained a BSc, she sees herself as an educated ragamuffin. She loves dancing, camping and acting. A recent achievement was when she won a local talent competition with her surprisingly realistic impression of a kookaburra.

Ruby's faith and outlook on life is reflected in her quirky observational writing.

ROSALIE ROSS

Rosalie Ross joined the Women's Royal Air Force at the age of seventeen where she trained as a nurse. Upon her discharge, and suffering from a bad case of wanderlust, she spent several years working as a casual seasonal worker in hotels and holiday camps in the Scottish Highlands and on England's East Coast.

She became a Christian at the age of twenty-eight and spent a year at a Methodist Bible College. Five years later, she settled down to marriage and children.

Always having felt the urge to write, her first book took her almost eleven years to complete – due to *life's ups-and-downs.* Her second book was completed soon after. She is currently working on her third.

Her motivation for writing, and her heartfelt desire, is that her work speaks to someone, somewhere, about the reality of God's love, and that they too will come to know Him as their Faithful Companion along life's uncertain paths.

Rosalie has written the following books:-

* The Hidden Path
* My High Tower

ROBYN CAIN

Robyn's writing dreams began in high school and came to fruition after she gained her Masters in Creative Writing.

Her books are set primarily in Cheshire. Her writing incorporates British and Asian cultures and is in a variety of genres. So far, under her belt, she has amassed a comprehensive collection of works in contemporary fiction, supernatural horror, crime thriller, and a collection of short stories published in India.

She loves most things creative, including baking, pickle making, crocheting, painting and keeping company with fellow writers. She also runs writing groups for all ages.

As well as short story collections, Robyn has written the following books:-

- Seven Stops
- A Fine Balance
- Goods By Hand
- Footsteps of Galatea
- Devil's Crochet

Printed in Poland
by Amazon Fulfillment
Poland Sp. z o.o., Wrocław